The Violet Needle

Stories from Iran

Mohsen Rezaei
Translations by the author

Fomite

Burlington, VT

This book was originally published in 2017 as
سوزن بنفش   by Neshaneh with drawings by
Amirhossein Rezaei, cover artist for this edition.
Thanks to him, and all those who helped to
create an English version of this book.

ISBN-13: 978-1-953236-10-4
Library of Congress Control Number: requested

Fomite
58 Peru Street
Burlington, VT 05401
www.fomitepress.com

To Badri Mesbahfar, Mehdi Amirkhanloo Henrik T. Torgersen and Hossein Mortezaeian Abkenar because of the hope and motivation they gave me.

Contents

I

II

III

I

Stairway to Success

The best thing in the world is Coke. I had always thought that Coke is amazing, and that that was completely true. As I grow older I become even more certain that having a clear path in life, or finding an incredible job, or even breaking bad habits and replacing them with good deeds and even the latest BMWs – which are widely sold – or the world's great writers, painters, designers and architects' masterpieces, none of that is worth more than a Coke.

But I had an unanswered question in my mind. Having an unanswered question in mind is painful in a way that can't be cured with any painkiller. The question is "Why is

Coke so successful?" One must really admit that no one or nothing has ever been as successful as Coke.

To research the answer to this question, I once met with a Coke. It invited me to a motel at the end of the main street, and I arrived there some minutes early. Something I found most interesting was its punctuality. I am always true to my word, so I was there five minutes early. But it arrived right on time – not a bit sooner or later. After shaking hands and saying hello, I asked the first question that popped into my mind: "Are you canned or bottled?" It answered me calmly, as if it was expecting such a question, "I am bottled." And I fell in love with it. Coke in a bottle is much better than Coke in a can. I can't really say why, but I like bottled Coke better. It is like comparing the importance of defense to offense – it's impossible. But one might have more fun with offense.

The only strange thing for me was why I was invited to a motel. Why not a hotel?

When we were climbing the stairs, it was looking at me in a way that made me think that soon I was going to be surprised. When we reached the door to a room, it cracked me up by saying, "I live in this room." That was unbelievable. The best thing in the world was living in a small room in a motel at the end of the main street and I didn't know that. Nobody knew! Did you? Did you know that?

Once the door was opened, the next surprise just blew my mind: aside from a heavy smell of cookies and a smooth smell of brown paper, there was nothing in the room but different books on road construction and various versions of "The Birdman of Alcatraz", on Betacam, VHS, DV, CD, DVD, Blue Ray, 8 mm, 16 mm, wide 16 mm, 35mm, and even 70 mm formats. The resolution on the 8 mm was less than the others, and the Super 16 mm's sound of course had the best quality.

I had come to find the answer to a single question, but by then I had thousands of new questions, and the Coke had answers for all of them. It turned to me and started to explain. The road construction books were to help it make roads. That was the weirdest answer to that question. It went on and said that all roads to success and improvement in this world are filled with passengers, and one had to build new roads in order to achieve any string of victories. I was thinking that was the biggest lesson of my life. I said: "I always used to think that cookies do not really go well with Coke," and it said what I was smelling was the smell of cookies it itself had cooked. And I, rude, frank, and curious, asked: "Well, are you a man or a housewife?" And I burst into laughter. It did not answer and I found out that it was a man because it laughed loudly too and was not shy at all. That discussion made us more intimate.

Suddenly I came to myself and told it excitedly that I would likely write a story about this meeting, which I guessed would be clichéd and banal, a story of a man who visited a Coke and found out its secrets of success. Then the Coke told me something that made me feel completely like a wet sack of cement. It said: "You haven't found out any secrets yet, kid!" And then it added: "Don't worry about your story, I'll fix that up right now." And it asked me to wear itself. I was relieved because nobody had ever heard a story of a man who dressed up as a Coke. After that, dressed as a Coke, I started to discover its secrets of success.

First, we went to a train station. Two busy, respectable women were waiting for the train, and seemed quite late and out of breath. The Coke said being on time is one of the most important things, and asked me to offer the ladies two bottles of Coke. I did so and the ladies were so happy seeing the Cokes that they acted ridiculous and jumped up and down with joy. They took the bottles and left the station burping. The Coke said, that is why people like Coke more than trains. After that we went to a big shot playwright's office.

The playwright was thinking about some way to end his play. But a problem like this is not something to be solved by thinking. The Coke said the second point is inattention. It paid no attention to the writer who was desperately hoping for help. Little by little the writer became attracted to the Coke swallowed a bit out of curiosity, and then he burnt all his plays in the fireplace. And I found out why people prefer Coke to plays. And the third instruction; "You need to be completely shameless!" That was what the Coke told me, and hearing this, I doubted my criteria for guessing its gender.

We went together to a diplomat who played a crucial role in international diplomacy. The Coke ordered the diplomat quite rudely "Hey, you! Come polish my shoes." The diplomat took a look, was delighted, and delicately, properly, polished the Coke's shoes. He gazed after us with a look full of kindness while we were getting away. This made me finally understand why people prefer Coke to politics.

But right at that moment the Coke told me something that made me as pale as a steamed bathroom mirror. It turned to me and said: "Now I have to tell you the secret of my success." I thought I had found out all about the Coke, but at that moment, I realized my mistake.

First, the Coke asked me to take my Coke off, which I did in a phone booth. After that, we set out walking together. But it was too far to walk. So first we took a taxi. Then we took the subway. After that, we got off the subway and walked a few kilometers. Then we took a taxi again, and when we got out, we were headed toward an old house. The Coke took a key from its pocket and opened the door. We entered a corridor, and after passing by a stairway, we reached a small living room. Suddenly an elderly voice said, "You home, son?" I saw the Coke's old mother in the corner of the living room, sitting in a wheelchair, and its father, older than she, lying sick in his bed. Its mother asked: "Would you take your father to the bathroom?" It answered cheerfully: "Sure, mom!" Tears came to my eyes. The Coke took its father to the bathroom and I sat in front of its mother, listening to some Shostakovich piece softly filling the room like a rumor. After they coming out of the bathroom, the Coke warmed up its mother's food and fed her patiently, spoon after spoon.

It was dark when we left its parents' house. The Coke told me it had to go back to its room at the motel and I, shocked, without saying a word, accompanied it. When we arrived at the motel, I wanted to leave, but the Coke asked me to go along with it to its room for a few minutes. So we did. It still smelled of cookies and brown paper. It first swallowed down some cookies and told me that it needed to fortify itself. It offered me cookies too, and I took one. Then it guided me to a closet and opened the door. That was something unbelievable. There was a stairway in the closet, heading up. The Coke started up the stairway and asked me to come along, and I, taking small, cautious steps, followed it. The more we climbed, the more stairs were left. When the stairs finally finished, my knees were completely numb, and we had reached some huge open space. I don't know what you think, but what I saw there was quite unimaginable. Hundreds of thousands of birds were sitting quietly, staring at me as I entered. I did not dare to go any further. The Coke said: "Don't worry, come on!" We went through the birds, who skipped out of our way. In the space there was a large machine in which brown paper came in from above and after being wetted down with sprinkles of Coke -- already fortified – were kneaded by massive gears into a dough, and were spit out at the bottom of the machine in tiny balls which were collected in a huge container. Those tiny balls were the birds' food. They fed from that food all night long, and in the morning, flew out in the air and pooped on people's heads. The poop, because of its acidity, was instantly absorbed in hair and scalp, and after getting into the bloodstream, reached a person's mind. Because they contained Coke's genetic information, they could affect a person's psyche, and as a result, the person fell in love with Coke. The bad thing was that the information was catching for their spouses and could affect the children as well.

That was how I realized Coke's secret of success. The next day I moved to a small village far away from the city. I rarely went out, and when I did, I wore a very thick hat. And I avoided birds. I never married and never again touched any Coke. But…but I remain sincerely in love with Coke.

Watching Kung Fu Panda

Once there was a person who was going to commit suicide. But his mind was busy with another thought; he had a cute toy he didn't know how to turn on, or how it worked. So he decided not to kill himself, before first understanding his toy. Then he would try suicide.

He traveled to different places, went everywhere, but nobody knew how to work the toy, because that toy was too ancient and old. At last he went to an " Expert In Toys That Nobody Knows How They Work ". This was a little old man who was partnering with his very rotten grandson. The old man knew newer toys because he had

Alzheimer's and didn't remember old ones, and his grandson was scrutinizing old toys and knew every unknowable thing about them. The person waited until they carefully looked the toy over, and waited for them to say something. "I've seen a toy like this before," the old man said. The person rejoiced. The old man continued, "But I don't remember anything about it." The grandson said that he had never seen such a thing even in history books, and he couldn't help the person except to guarantee him something.

Guarantee!

It was most interesting for the person, because this guarantee was not so simple, but very complicated. The person was assured by the grandson that his toy was very, very valuable, and most probably was the same amazing toy mentioned in history as the " Problem Solver ". The person rejoiced to hear this, forgot suicide completely, and decided to spend the rest of his life using the toy to solve all of his problems in life.

After that, he took the toy with him everywhere and asked everyone about it. Once, somebody told him that the cylinder in the stomach of the toy might turn. The person turned the cylinder and enjoyed its warm squeak. It was from that moment on that turning the cylinder focused his mind, and he tried to understand the workings of the toy via this turning. He traveled all over the world again and met Steven Edwards, Alison Angel, Abu Shayeq Hakami, Jean-Claude Van Damme, Hesam Habibi, Vintage Castle, Maria Full of Grace, The Man Who Knew Too Much, and Charlton Heston. Charlton Heston suggested that he watch the animated film "Kung Fu Panda", and the person felt a light wiggling in his stomach. After watching "Kung Fu Panda", he concluded that nobody could help him except himself and that he alone was the only one who could help him. So he decided to play with the toy till he know how it worked. The idea that only he could figure it out, the feeling of being useful, brought him back to life.

One day, after many calculations, he concluded something interesting: next to the cylinder there was a thick metal pipe with something like a small petal stuck to its edge. And under the cylinder there was a small metal piece – something like an almond slice. The person held the pipe right in front of his mouth, and after turning the cylinder and enjoying its sound, he moved the almond-slice-metal-piece – and with a bang, a quite hot cartridge jumped into his mouth, passed through his throat and uvula, blood and neurons, and hit the wall. A soft pale smoke rose up from the toy, along with a strange odor.

The Mountain of the Estate

Ever wonder what would happen if people had gills? it must be said in that case, things would be just as they are now. The truth is that people initially had gills. All of them were living underwater, unable to imagine the world outside. People were simply living their underwater lives, and had no trouble. They were just like today's people, but imagine in that ballet mécanique, instead of hands and legs, they had fish-eye lenses instead of eyes. The only distinguishing difference in comparison with current people was they were ignoramuses. Actually, it was the best thing for them, but it did not last long.

Among the gill-people there was a gill-woman called Marjan[1]. The reason they called her Marjan was simple; initially she was a coral except for the special courage she revealed, and because in spite of being a coral she was very soft, and could trans-form into a gill-person in social situations. However, some people believed her father was a gill-man and her mother was a cliff, but she herself had always said these were rumors, and not true. Anyway, whatever she was, she was slightly - only very, very slight-ly – wise. For instance, she had concluded many times that there was another world out of the water that others didn't know about, and that when people died, they would go to the out-of-the-water world and live there. She also had theories about calculating the speed of light in water and the pressure of one cubic foot of water at its base. But her worst theory was that she thought she had to gather together riches for her life

---

1 Marjan is a feminine name in Persian. It also means "Coral".

after death. She stored everything she got, she stacked everything up, she heaped her goods until they made a mountain.

One day Marjan climbed the mountain to put a few pairs of underwear and bras up at the top so that when she would leave this world, they would be accessible, and she would not have to look for them. When she got to the top of her riches-mountain, she found its peak was protruding up above the water. She realized that was the boundary between the water and the world-out-of-it. So she grew curious, and lifted her head out. She had not put her underwear on yet, and so the air blew through her gills and filled her with a joy she had never known before. But after a while she felt choked, put her bra over her mouth, breathed in the water left in her bra, and looked around. Suddenly, something weird attracted her attention, but since she had too little water to breathe, she felt dizzy and fell down the mountain into the depth of water. When she came to again, she was so excited that she called people together and tried as hard as she could to make them realize what had happened to her out of the water. But people were dimwitted, and didn't get it. She concluded that nobody would understand her. On the other hand, the temptation of getting out of the water still remained.

Since women cannot resist their desires, and because Marjan was somewhat wise, she made a water capsule for herself, climbed the mountain again, and stuck her head out. She looked around too, and enjoyed it. That weird thing drew her attention once more. She raised her capsule and called out "What kind of thing are you?" and instantly put it back on. The thing ran to Marjan at one fifth of the speed of light, and said, " I'm Redskin." "How do you run on water?" Marjan asked, and immediately put her mask back on. "I've gotten this far by meditating." Then he said to Marjan with eyes filled with love, "Let's go to America together." Marjan asked for some time to think about it. Since she was somewhat wise, she thought for a while and imagined the future. She imagined America with its redskins and concluded they were some primitive and naive people, pleased with their rituals, and then she thought she could wipe them out and revolutionize America. She imagined a glorious picture of the future New York and answered Redskin, "I'll come with you."

Yes, they got married – and all of us are the children of Redskin and Marjan. If today, we can breathe without a water capsule and have no gills, it is inherited from our father, and if we are greedy creatures and have only a little wisdom, that is from our mother. Perhaps one day a pure redskin will be born again, or maybe a pure coral Marjan who is soft of course. However, I guess the race of gill-people will never re-emerge.

Der blaue Reiter

Come sit down here. I want to tell you the story of the Timers. There is no relation at all between the Timers and time. They were just people who lived long ago. Timers were the only humans whose width was greater than their length. That would apply to everything about them: the width of their body was greater than its length, the width of their lifetime was greater than its length, and many other things. Timers had interesting behaviors. For instance, in wars they dug huge trenches called khandaqs, which have inspired the Arabs.

War

In one of the wars, some were responsible

for digging the trenches. When the enemy army was getting close, the trenches were quickly made deeper. The ones who stood outside the trenches were encouraging, and there were more of them. Those in the trenches were working hard, and never raised their heads. As the enemy arrived, the Timers above looked back at the mountain, and one of them whistled. Another Timer was standing on the mountain, and when he heard the whistle, he cut several ropes with a big knife, releasing huge stones which rolled downhill. The Timers above stepped aside, and the huge stones passed in front of them and rolled down into the trench. Everybody down there was buried under the stones. The enemy arrived and climbed up on the stones. The surviving Timers smiled, and made a treaty of friendship.

In addition, Timers were so evolved as to play electronic games, and though they did not know much about it, they are now considered the pioneers of electronics. On the other hand, their childish games led them to invent a device called a resonator. But they used the resonators as baby diapers. Some other interesting things about them: it was the Timer style in making peace and signing contracts that the Romans and Greeks adopted for their own administrative and political systems.

Peace

The Timers that had stayed out of the trenches became friends with their enemies. In fact, they already had such a plan in advance, because unlike them, enemies' lengths were more than their widths and they could have an additive life next to one another. Every male timer got married to an enemy female, and their wedding photos show bride (|) and groom (–) and when they kissed one another, they became like a plus sign (+). Timers in their short lifetime on earth made peace with all their enemies and eliminated many friends to achieve this goal. The male Timers died so soon that earth became overrun by their widows. The male Timers built huge palaces for their wives and painted most intricately all the cities under their rule. Everything was covered with arabesques; even trees leaves, and lactating women's breasts, and the pebbles that accumulated at the mouths of ant nests. Their painting style had much effect on the Harat and Tabriz schools, and also the works of der blaue Reiter.

Timers never went through alleys. They walked in the streets; alleys were for people who were not Timers. That was because their width was more than their length, and their traffic would make trouble. That's why wide streets were constructed — so that Timers could get around easily. In archaeological digs, some streets wider than modern high-ways and even freeways have been found, and it is said that Timers walking in those streets would take their entire width. That's why all streets were one-way. As the ratio of their width to their length were all the same, they depended on their long-lived wives — who were all from the enemies' race — to continue their reign, though it was fruitless and sterile.

Reign

When the Timers died and their widows remained on earth, they extended the Timers' reign. But because women always bring their personal ideas into governing and those people were no exception, nothing remains from the era of the Timers' reign. But as examples of Timers' widows' styles, some unique literary works were created such as A Thousand And One Nights, and Forty Parrots. The widows governed for thousands of years. All modern women stem from Timers' widows. They gave birth with each other's help, and their behavior initiated lesbianism. Male Timers believed in having their wives involved in their personal lives. That's why they did not allow them to interfere in government. They believed their wives were useful for nothing except giving birth, and in some other things like killing off the ancient ways of speaking, and creating philosophical and ontological attitudes which, after the Timers' death, were all proven correct. The last Timer was killed by his wife's hand. Timers also used to eat mushroom soup, and what we have today as the history of Timers has been written by their wives.

Threads

Nobody thinks about the things a needle does in a sewing box: nothing. But I mean a violet needle. Violet needles are specific. If there is no sewing, there is nothing for a needle to do. But a violet needle has an identity apart from sewing because it is able to make decisions, and this power distinguishes it from the others. It's wrong to suppose there is a thread among other threads that is similar to the violet needle. Threads are all the same and have no color. Only the supplies have colors, especially needles.

The violet needle is famous as Mahmud. In the sewing box, it is always adored by the other supplies – thimbles, spools, bobbins, scissors and even sewing machine needles (sewing machine needles are affiliated with the machine, and even have no thread without the machine. But the violet needle is always paired with a thread of unlimited length that tides it over. The thread always wants to go into the needle's eye and has no other choice.)

You may often have seen these needles, but don't remember, because they look different. Maybe once you went to a restaurant and a young waitress asked "Anything else I can get you?" and you've answered "Nothing". And then she made some suggestions – salad, shallot yogurt, cool carbonated drinks, processed olives, a pickle, French fries … and with her special skill she has gotten you to order all of them. And in the end, you notice the add-ons have cost more than the main course. You may have eaten your food and left the restaurant without realizing that the waitress was a violet needle.

Maybe you have gone to a dentist to

pull an aching tooth and get rid of it. But, instead, the dentist filled your tooth and warned you about more cavities, and then filled all of them. You left with filled teeth, but they all have been constantly aching, keeping you up at night. You never understood that the dentist filled your teeth with a violet needle.

Violet needles play many roles in society. Many cinemas have violet needles on screen instead of films, and many of you grow violet needles in flower pots in your house. Most teachers are in fact violet needles. Shoes that don't hurt your feet and you are so comfortable with them; songs that are produced and published at enormous cost, and you are their big fan; people who sometimes accidently bump into you in the street and turn back and apologize politely; pasta sauce that you buy at the store and heat and add to pasta at the last moment to put on dining table … All of them are violet needles you are not aware of.

But if a violet needle is so unrecognizable, how does one distinguish it from others?[2] It is said in history that once a tailor – very unexpectedly – quietly entered his workshop and went to the sewing box. As he opened it, he saw the violet needle teaching strange things to the other supplies – all of which listened with even more respect than they gave to the tailor. The violet needle noticed the tailor but didn't feel guilty. When the tailor tried to shout, it jumped out and began sewing the tailor's lips together with the thread that was always threaded through its eye. The tailor was going to run for help, but the violet needle sewed his feet to the ground with astonishing speed, so no one could see. It closed the door, sewed it to the frame, and on a large piece of material, embroidered a

---

2 Surely you know that when tailors enter their workshops, they always make a lot of noise, and the supplies in the supply box notice, and when the box is opened, they act as if nothing has happened in the box since the last time it was opened.

likeness of the tailor at work, and installed it behind the window so people would think the tailor was doing his job as usual. But there was one very intelligent cop who figured out all these were fake and, in an exciting adventure, undid all the sewing and saved the tailor so he could explain everything. That was how the violet needle came to be known. But if you want the truth, the cop was not so intelligent. He was only a violet needle. Because only violet needles know each other's business.

Baqareh-ei Fish

You should never underestimate an Icelander. An Icelander splits a mountain with his hands and rolls the earth under his feet and his eyes are filled with a sea of blood and two Baqareh-ei fish live beneath its waves. Baqareh-ei fish is a kind of fish which eats like a cow; yogurt and cheese are made from its milk. And villagers use Baqareh-ei fish to plow their farms and grow wheat, corn, Armenian cucumber and Brazilian tomatoes. Brazilian tomatoes are still green when they are taken by big trucks to different places, and they turn red when they are delivered, like girls who have put on rouge. Especially Bijan rouge.

Bijan was a successful Iranian-American man who is no longer alive. The best cosmetics in the world were produced for many years under the name of Bijan in his factory. A lot of women use this brand when they go to fancy parties, laughing, dancing, getting men in the sack, and finally, reclining exhausted, too tired to wash off their makeup. They just wipe their faces with tissues and throw them away. Tissues are poor things. They are united and glorious initially, but become folded and put in little cardboard boxes. They sleep on each other and they are taken out singly and dirtied. Finally, they are tossed away like a comet. A comet is also a poor thing. It is thrown out inadvertently and breaks up on the ground.

Once there was a young man who had just met a young woman. Both were divorced, and each had a child with their ex-spouse. They fell in love. They had just understood the real meaning of love.

They got married. Their children each gained another sibling and they sprouted, grew up, and got more and more beautiful, like small plants. The family decided to leave their crowded city, move to a distant place, and live in a quiet, peaceful atmosphere. They all packed up their things and moved to a small village on a riverbank, a village which had only one school, a few houses and a lot of beautiful countryside. The sound of the river was the music of their life. And the children were growing up as healthy and shiny as jungle fruits. They built a tree house, a big wooden house, they made a slide, a swing, a Ferris wheel in the yard surrounded by trees. And a big log table and chairs. The family often had meals there.

At lunch one cool day, the young man turned to his wife and looked at her affectionately. The woman hugged the children while staring amorously at the man. One of the children looked at his mother and said,

"Mommy!" the mother answered kindly, "Yes, dear?" the child pointed at the sky and asked, "What's that?" the mother looked up, and just then a big comet hit them, and killed them all, and destroyed their belongings. They were buried under the giant comet forever.

The comet had to do it. It didn't mean to do it. But the comets are really unaware. They don't know what is going to happen. They don't know what's up next. But the truth should be told. No one knows what is going to happen. No one is sure about the past, let alone today or tomorrow. But I dare say an Icelander knows. An Icelander shouldn't be underestimated. His eyes are filled with a sea of blood, and two Baqareh-ei fish live in its waves. I'm going to tell you the story of Baqareh-ei fish.

II

Sulfuric Acid

There once was a married couple who had lived together until the husband got a stomach ache. After an examination, the doctor told him that a bear lived in his stomach. When the husband asked, "How is that possible?" He answered, "Bears live wherever comfort is provided." "Then what should I do?" the husband asked. "Surgery," the doctor answered. The husband and wife were upset, and the suffering husband took his wife's hand and returned home.

At midnight, the husband woke up and could not speak. In fact, he could not make any sound at all, because a periscope had come out of his mouth. The husband was afraid of waking his wife up, because she might have a panic attack. "This is the voice of the bear," said a voice from the periscope. The husband could only respond by eye motion. "You better not go for surgery," the voice said, and then began to speak mysterious words, revealing secrets about the universe. The man and the bear made a pact: the bear would tell the man the secrets of the universe, and the man would abstain from surgery.

During the following days, the man ate only what the bear wanted, and the bear let him in on everything. But his wife was insistent that he go for an operation. The husband enjoyed his universal knowledge, and his stomach ache seemed not as important as before. One day, the bear explained to the husband that nothing except good lasts in this world, and everything the man has which is not good sticks on to the good like a smear.

The husband decided to sell all he had:

house, car, bag, shoes and clothes, bank shares, and everything – everything except what was good. To stop her husband, the wife said, "I'm pregnant." the husband was overjoyed at this news. To him, however, nothing was as important as knowledge, and when the bear asked him to cook him up a great meal, he did so. In return, the bear said, he would reveal a deep secret about his wife.

The bear, after eating a fatty, delicious meal, instructed the husband to divorce his wife as soon as possible. The husband could not accept that, but the bear told him that this was one of the smears. The husband was not satisfied with this response so, though the meal was not enough to reveal two secrets at the same time, the bear agreed to reveal yet another deep secret. The husband waited to hear what the bear had to say. The bear said, "Your wife has a bear cub in her womb." The husband seethed with rage, divorced his wife, and later received an envelope. In it, there was a picture of his wife holding a fat, white baby boy, and the husband realized his wife did not have a bear cub in her womb after all. In his rage, without thinking further, he decided to punish the bear in his stomach, so he drank a four-liter jug of sulfuric acid and died instantly. The bear tore open the stomach of the dead husband, jumped out, went to a diner, and hid himself in a hamburger bun.

Cops

One million years ago, there was a little girl who made days of the week into sculptures and put them up for sale in the city's main sculpture market. Before buying sculptures, people went back to the calendar, counted their lost days and sighed. Then they checked their pockets to see how much money they had, went to the sculpture market and bought sculptures of the lost days from the little girl who had made them, and so could do their undone works in her sculptures. It was really beneficial for them. Some people married off their housekeepers' daughters, some watched soccer matches they had missed, some made up absences at meetings. But not in the real days – only in the sculptures of those days.

The little girl had been doing her thing with no problems for five hundred and twenty thousand years, till one day – that is four hundred and eighty thousand years before now – a man came to her and asked for the statue of Tuesday, the 27th of three months ago. The little girl walked among the statues and came back empty-handed. The man did not want to hear it, but he was told that Tuesday, the 27th of three months ago was not available. The little girl browsed through the statues again, but the day the man wanted had been sold. Although the girl was sorry, the man grabbed up some sculptures and smashed them cruelly on her head. The little girl wondered what was going on. She asked him why that day was so important to him, and the man said he had murdered someone on the 27th of three months ago, and he had been hiding out all this time and was so tense. He wanted the statue of that day so he could undo the murder, and be free of the crime. The little girl said the statue had been sold, but she gave the man the address of the buyer.

The man looked for the buyer for twenty thousand years till he found him under a phone booth four hundred and sixty thousand years ago. He was a full-scale clockwork doll with sequins constantly flashing, and a finger pointing fixedly at the sky. The man asked him many questions, but the doll was not tuned up, so it didn't answer. The man did not notice that, so he beat the doll with his fists, but learned nothing. He took the beaten doll to a repairman of full-scale clockwork dolls. The repairman told him he had to tune up the doll, that the man should leave the doll with him, and come back in three thousand years. The man came back to the repairman right on time, four hundred and fifty-seven thousand years ago, and heard that the doll had been repaired and re-tuned, but could not speak.

The man stressed that he could wait as many thousand years as were needed until the doll could speak so it could reveal the location of the statue of the 27th of three months before twenty-three thousand years ago. But the repairman said that even if he waited billions of years, this doll could not speak, because it was not a talking doll. It only could vibrate its finger and point toward the sky. That was the only thing it could do. The man was completely disappointed, but the repairman mentioned an interesting point. He said full-scale clockwork dolls hide everything they buy under phone booths. The man remembered he had found the doll under a phone booth. But there were forty-two million phone booths in that city. The man remembered the phone booth had been on 31st street. But that was useless too because there were forty-three million 31st streets in that city. The man had no choice but to go to a boothologist. The boothologist found the booth for the man in only one hundred and twenty years and dug under it. But there was nothing. The boothologist discovered that the statue had burrowed down and escaped. So both of them went down into the burrow to try to catch the statue while it was trying to get away.

The little girl in her booth sold the sculpture of the day, and as she turned back to put the money in the cash box, she saw a hole in the ground and the statue of the 27th of three months before twenty-three thousand and one hundred and twenty years ago coming up from the hole. She picked it up and studied it. It was so old, it no longer seemed useful. So she cut it into as many pieces as she could, and threw it into the ruined-statues bucket. After a while the man and the boothologist came up from the hole. The man was happy to see the little girl, and asked about the statue. The little girl told him what had happened. The man became most impatient and angry. The boothologist remained calm, and suggested that he buy today's statue to prevent its events. The little girl said she has sold that statue to a full-scale clockwork doll a few minutes ago. At that moment the cops charged into the statue market and swarmed all over. After much violence, they arrested the man and took him with them.

Summer

I'm sure you will all blame this man. The man with his big suitcases in hand who is leaving his house forever, and is not trying to stay and take back the house. But this is the end of the adventure. You don't know what happened. Nothing was this man's fault. Drinking water was his fault. Yes, he would drink water only from the water dispenser on his fridge. Perhaps it would have been better to use a smaller glass. A big Chinese mug sat near the water dispenser and the man used to fill it to the brim. But he always left a quarter mug undrunk. Who would think that to be such a terrible thing?

Every time he went for a drink, he

poured the water remaining from previous time into the small flower pot beside the fridge. Indeed, it was the only thing he did. Only an eye as sharp as an eagle's, an ear keen as a wolf's, or a nose as sensitive as a dog's would have noticed during one of those pourings the presence of an ant on its way somewhere in the flower pot near the stem, scanning all around with its antennae with no clear aim. If you had asked the man, he would have said "a little water." but from the ant's point of view it was "a horrible flood" that engulfed it and washed it into the dirt.

The ant died, but its curse was alive. In its last moments, it had cursed the cause of that flood from its very heart. It is extremely dangerous to survive a curse. You will understand – even dinosaurs surviving would not threaten you more than a curse, if one day a curse should follow you.

The ant's curse caused its heart to crack, and a black stalk grew out of it. An ant flesh stalk came out of the soil, black, shiny, with small sticky hairs. That stalk – just like private banks – developed countless branches, with fruit hanging from each, swaying, and trying with all their might to fall from the branch. Angry ants were the fruits of that new-grown tree, the tree the man helped grow with a quarter mug of water every day. I believe this was his only sin: habitually doing something without thinking or attention. He routinely watered this black sapling for a long time without noticing that it had been cracking, breaking and its dirt had been moving into the kitchen. He didn't even see the big black tree contrasting so starkly with the white fridge.

Finally, one day, one of those angry ants became so ripe and juicy it could separate itself from the tree. That marked the beginning of harvest season. Gradually, ants could separate from the tree and meander randomly all over the kitchen floor and furniture and walls and – just like that eternal curser – have no goal and shake their antennae – all except for those who were still a little immature.

I thought the mug itself must have been filled with ants instead of water, by the time the man realized what had happened to him. It was only then that he saw his house had become overrun by ants – as if it was made entirely of ants. You surely won't guess his reaction. Since he was a very law-oriented person, quite unemotional, he cooly went to court and sued the ants. Having a savvy lawyer is useful in such cases. But he wanted to be fair, and to simply respect the law. I have to say he did right, because no friend or lawyer could do much to help with that case, because even the law supported the ants. The ants had the opportunity to become a part of the environment, and doing anything against them was considered an attack on the environment. But humans are not part of the environment, especially men, especially a lonely man.

The court concluded, "As ants are older than humans, and the whole earth is their home, it is the man who is occupying their property with his body and his destructive occupying appliances – including a refrigerator that makes cold water over and over again."

Respectful of the law, the man hung his head and returned to his house. From a distance, it looked black and shapeless. As he approached, the ants quieted down and stopped roughhousing. The house was no more. They had broken the entire house down to particles that could be stored under the soil for the cold days of winter.

On the Rings

Please note! There was a fuzzy man who had lost everything. He had nothing. It is hard for anyone to imagine somebody who has nothing – pay attention: NOTHING. He was not like that at the beginning. On the contrary, he had everything. It's so hard to believe that somebody might have every-thing – pay attention: EVERYTHING. But Fuzzy Man had everything and lost every-thing, so he became completely poor. But at the peak of poverty, one thing remained to him. There was one thing he still hadn't lost. And that was "himself". Fuzzy Man had himself. It was the only thing left.

Until, in cold weather, at a point on the

earth tangent to Jupiter, a blue man came around, and decided to buy Fuzzy Man's self. Fuzzy Man was completely unwilling to sell himself. He thought of that as "prostitution". But Blue Man corrected him, said that prostitution was something else, and showed Fuzzy Man some potential weakness in his ideology. It might be interesting for him to sell this last remaining thing in his life. It was exciting for him to imagine what lay afterward.

Still, he decided to consult with others. He knew nobody but flute's tune. He approached the flute and heard its strange whining and complaining about separations. Scrutinizing him, he found the flute like this: a thin and hollow creature aloof from all the world, seeking emancipation and freedom. It was the best advice: if Fuzzy Man would sell himself, he would reach perfect freedom.

Immediately, at some place on the earth similar to the huts of Mercury, he met Blue

Man and told him he had agreed to the deal. Blue Man reddened with gladness, laughed out loud, and his eyes shone. But what should Fuzzy Man exchange himself for? No matter how much he thought, nothing came to mind – until Blue Man suggested something he accepted. What was the suggestion?

Blue Man took Fuzzy Man's self, and, in return, gave him a gleam of hope. A gleam of hope is a very good thing. In fact, this gleam is a tight small hole that, on its other side, shows what a man doesn't have. If someone looks from this side of the hole to the other, he would become very hopeful.

Fuzzy Man's self had become Blue Man's, and on the other side of the deal there was an owned-without-owner called gleam of hope. Thereafter, Fuzzy Man won lottery prizes, and the most beautiful girls from all over the world wanted to marry him, penetrating eyes, harp-player fingers, and flexible joints were eager to be his own.

But there was no Fuzzy Man anymore; whatever he was, he was a blue man, a blue man who has everything, everything…and everybody wanted to be with him, everybody wanted to belong to him, and nobody wanted to leave him alone. The gleam of hope, finding nobody to look from this side to the other, ran freely along the rings of Saturn, and started to skip.

The Shorthaired Man

Early Sunday morning they brought a longhaired man and installed him in the center of the crossroad, put a rope around his neck, pulled tight, and nailed it to the ground. A boy tied a bow tie on his neck, and when the boy wanted to take it back, the longhaired man pointed to the bow tie, and the boy got scared and disappeared.

Cars that wanted to pass the crossroad were forced to drive around the longhaired man, and women tried to look down so nobody could notice their excitement. Sweepers could no longer sleep all night and sweep quickly in the early morning. They swept all night long, and there were no floozies hanging around. The crossroad cops were forced to fine all offenders, and could not take bribes. Since the longhaired man was there all day and night, there were many things done, and those undone had to be done stealthily. As stealthy business increased, gold, housing, Fender guitars, Peugeots, Japanese seeds, toilets, Oral-B toothbrushes, DVDs, and everything else became more expensive – so expensive that people walked bent over. But to keep their pride they tried to stand still before the longhaired man, and stood there even with all the trouble they felt; it was that important for them. Once somebody jumped off the highest building of the town, and everybody said he did that for the longhaired man. Prices continued to increase, and people thought of hoarding. Everything got hoarded: cash, clothes, body strength, oil, food, sperm, good deeds… the people even stopped up toilets to save their stool and urine.

One day, the boy felt he should put on his bow tie to go to music class – but he remembered it was tied to the longhaired man's neck. He went to the crossroad and saw the longhaired man standing there, not pointing to the bow tie. The boy untied his bow tie and as he was turning back home, a wolfpack attacked the longhaired man, and one of them pulled his rope from the ground. The boy ran up, pulled the rope back, and spiked it in the ground again so longhaired man wouldn't fall. The people noticed the wolves, and though they were very weak, they struggled with them. But the wolves easily overpowered the people. One of the wolves attacked the boy. The longhaired man saw the wolf tear the boy's body up, and because of what the boy had done for him, he wanted save him any way he could. But there was nothing to do because he was not real, he was only nailed together.

Early Sunday morning they picked up

the longhaired man from the center of the crossroad and put a shorthaired man in his place. There was no need to use a rope, because the shorthaired man was built as one piece based on statics so he could stand by himself.

Lemur-in-Clothing

You probably have heard about the man who had a lemur living in his clothing. Some said he had been a practicing magician for many years and the lemur was leftover from that time. Now the man was a hotel owner, but the lemur was not giving up. Of course, the man himself said many times he hadn't kept a lemur during his time as a magician, but that was disproven. Once at a party in an empty room, as soon as the zipper came down, the lemur poked his head out and the poor lady jumped out of the bag, screaming.

This lemur made too many troubles. The man understood he could not live that way anymore. He thought about how he might get rid of it, and at last he found an interesting solution: the lemur was living in the man's clothes, and at night, when he took off his clothes and went to bed, the lemur slept in his clothes like some adorable little kid. The man figured that without clothes, there would be no lemur. So he decided not to wear clothes anymore. The next day, the man went out of house completely naked, and people's amazed looks, old women's glares, old men's sneers, little boys' laughter, and little girls' muffled screams were all more tolerable than the lemur. It was the first day of relief after many years of lemur-in-clothing.

But the next day, the story changed. The street in front of the hotel filled with people who, with various excuses, had come to see a completely naked man with a perfectly polite, dignified attitude. The hotel filled with people from one or two blocks away, and the shameless presence in public of a hotel owner without even a pair of socks – one with a great background in magic tricks – was not a trivial event for journalists and photographers. As soon as the news got around, the Law arrived and arrested the man for disruption of social order and custom, cultural upheaval, unconventional behavior, and creating chaos at the social, cultural, political and economic level, and also working with terrorist and spy groups to shatter the foundations of national security. The man stood up before the Law, and politely explained everything. The Law understood the man's misery, but ordered him to find another way to save himself. It signed a release, ordered him back in his clothes with the lemur, and left him free to return to his usual life.

The man left a message after the beep: "Hey, Dude! I need your help". And at night, a huge, dark gentleman rang his doorbell. The man gladly opened the door and squeezed his visitor into the house.

They consulted all night about the man's problem. The huge, dark gentleman was a heavyweight boxer whose punches would leave nothing standing, only a forgotten memory. His pummeling could return anything back to the time before it existed. But he had never been prepared for aggression against some weak creature like that lemur. The only help he offered was a promise to train both the man and the lemur in boxing, so they could face one another in a perfectly honest fight until one overcame the other. For the next few days the man and the lemur were training and exercising under the coach's expert supervision.

The fight day came. A huge crowd rushed to see the epic battle. The man was all ready, waiting to enter the ring. The fight organizer came in, looked angrily at the man and said, "What's going on? Why aren't you ready?" the man answered that he was quite ready. But the organizer meant why was he completely naked? And the man explained. But it was impossible for the organizer to allow a naked boxer in the ring. The dark gentleman coach encouraged the man to accept the rules and not to disqualify himself. But the man jumped in the ring nevertheless, at the same time as the lemur. They were one soul - excuse me - two souls in one body; the lemur had gotten completely comfortable in the man's boxing shorts and was going to fight from inside them.

The fight began; the man was punching, and the lemur was dodging, and the man's knockdown punches were inevitably hitting himself. The lemur's relentless punches were hammering at the two points it had prepared as if pounding a punching bag. And the man, as any actual man would, lost to those continuous punches, and the multitudinous crowd was happily rooting for the lemur.

But this adventure was long ago. So much time passed by. The man lived years and years with the lemur in his clothes until at last, the dead body of the lemur fell out of his trouser leg. Since that day, the man has been lonely, even though living with a sword he had swallowed to the handle. Some say he had been a magician many years ago and the sword was left over from that time, but he himself disagrees.

Lawn Pot

Once upon a time there was a Lawn Man. He himself was not a lawn mower, but he had a machine that was a lawnmower. He was living on a globe that was covered by lawn and there was nothing except lawn; no bare lands, no basins, no lakes. There was not enough space for mountains or seas — the globe was too small. Every day, as he left the house, the Lawn Man, would watch the sun rise from below the arc-shaped horizon, and when it was sunny, he would pick up his machine and began to mow.

The lawns usually ignored him, because his job worked against them. But the man was fair; he used to work slowly, and sometimes paused so the lawns could breed, and then he turned around again and mowed them. The worst thing was when he went to the underside of the globe, because the globe was near the earth and the gravity of the earth caused the blood to pool in his head and gave him a headache.

One day, no matter what he could do, the machine stopped running. The lawnmower was badly damaged, and the man didn't know how to fix it. The lawns said "We can see from here that one of the gears is broken and must be changed." The man's troubles had just begun. He had to go to the earth to find the gear. But as he had never before gone anywhere, and was afraid of travelling, he sent a message to the earth asking someone to bring him the gear. For a few days he had nothing to do, and the lawns got so far ahead that the poor man went into the house so they would feel more comfortable.

Finally, a courier arrived from the earth

with the gear. The courier was astonished at seeing such a huge swath of lawn and the lawns were astonished at seeing a new man. "Are you a lawn man?" the lawns asked. "No," the courier answered, and that was strange for the lawns.

The machine was fixed, and started to work again. Several days passed same as always, until one day, as the man came out of the house at sunrise, he saw three elongated shadows rising on the curve of the horizon, and getting shorter moment by moment. When it was fully day, he saw three lawn men, each equipped with a lawnmower. "Who are you?" the Lawn Man asked. "We have come from the earth to help you. The courier told us there is too much lawn here." The man said, "I can do the job myself," but the lawn men didn't care, and began their work with speed and accuracy; job satisfaction broke out on their heads like sweat. It turned out they were getting a good wage.

The lawn found itself lagging behind,

so it started to work hard and multiplied its activity. But a few days later, three more came from the earth and joined the previous comers. The lawn lost hope. The Lawn Man was filled with pity for it. He put his machine aside and stayed in the house. He had collected a bit of lawn in a small pot and had taken it to the house to keep with him.

Eventually, the lawn men's non-stop work was over. The globe was completely bare. In photos, it didn't look like a green ball anymore; it had become a brown-earth ball. In future days, other people came from the earth – builders, architects, simple workers and complicated workers, school builders, road constructors, plumbers, shoe dealers, athletes, war heroes…and soon the globe was covered by humans and buildings.

The Lawn Man had to go out and buy another pot, because the lawn was breeding and increasing day by day. The pot seller, who could not understand the lawn man's business, once followed him, found what was going on, and refused to sell pots to the Lawn Man thereafter.

A few days later, when the lawn woke up, it found itself in a suitcase with its pot. It saw Lawn Man closing the suitcase, and then the lawn was plunged into darkness. The suitcase shook, the lawn felt itself moving, but it didn't understand where it was going.

Horn

Tying my laces, I told myself I couldn't stand it anymore, I had to buy new shoes. These were really hurting my feet. They needed softening up. I took a look at my watch; fuck! It was late! I picked up my bag and quickly left my apartment. I almost fell on the staircase two or three times. I thought I'd better not rush, so I took the stairs more slowly. On the last landing, I saw that Jamlian had put his foot up and was tying his shoelaces. I said hello: "How are you Mr. Jamlian?" "Good, thanks! And you?" he answered. "It's better to put your foot up on the stairs when you tie your shoes, no?" He looked at me and gave me a meaningless smile. He called after me as I was going down and said: "Excuse me, I'm Jamali, not Jamlian." I nodded, smiled and went on.

I got to the front steps. Kids were going to school. They all looked alike. Their clothes were all the same. I used to see them all the time. They were like that every day. I noticed how small they were! And as I was walking down the alley next to them, I was thinking how much stronger I was when I was their age, and that school kids were flashier even a few years ago. I looked at my watch. I couldn't believe that the hand had gotten to 4; twenty minutes passed!? I walked faster and gradually began to run. I got to the street. I was hurried enough to take a regular taxi and not wait for a Peugeot. But there was no time to think about it. I flagged one down and jumped in. My head kept bumping against the ceiling as we drove along. I thought to myself that's why I always wait for a Peugeot.

With this delay, I was wondering when

I would get to work, and was still wondering when I arrived. It was so interesting for me, because the street was not empty. I ran toward the office building, entered through the security door, and told the guard: "Find a way to fix the door." The guard took a look and said, "Hello!" I did not answer him and just got on the elevator. I was looking for the 7 button. Seven…seven…Where is the seven!? I said that, and got out and asked the guard: "Has the elevator panel been replaced?" "Yes," he said. "So why doesn't it have a seven?" "Why should it?" he said. Because I can't climb to the seventh floor," I said. He looked derisively at me, which made me try to look tougher, but it did not affect him. He asked me with a delicate grin, "What seventh floor do you mean?" "What do you mean?" I asked. "I mean we have only six floors here," he said. "My office is on the seventh floor," I said. He laughed and said, "I guess you didn't have breakfast." I could not figure out this remark.

I walked toward the staircase and climbed quickly. Two or three times I almost fell on my face. I thought I'd better not rush. I passed the floors one by one. I saw my office as I got to the sixth floor. I was so angry that they had changed my office without permission. Karimi was walking toward the end of the corridor with a tea tray in his hand. I called him. He turned back and came over, rubbing his shoes on the floor. "Hello," he said. "When did they change my office?" I asked. "Nobody has changed it," he said. "Now how can I get the key?" I asked. "Why are you so angry early in the morning? Don't you have a key?" he asked. "I do, but I have my mine," I said. He looked me in the eyes and said, "Then that's it." I continued looking for the key in my pockets: "The fucking lock is too small. Look at my key…" I said. I took out the key. "… It's too large to fit in the lock." Then I put the key up against the lock so he understood they were mismatched. But I saw they were matched. The key slipped smoothly into the lock so it was not as large as I thought. This was very mysterious! I looked at Karimi, and he looked at me with a comforting paternal smile and left.

I opened the door, bent down and entered. How small everything was! My desk, my computer, my room window. It all was the same as I had seen yesterday. The same but smaller. I walked toward the desk. I tried to sit down on the chair but it was too small, and I could not fit. I looked at my watch – two hours had passed. How could two hours have passed since I was talking to Jamlian? Not Jamlian, but Jamali…Jamali! I walked toward the window to take a look at the street. But I could see only as far as the fourth floor of the opposite building, not below that. I put my head out the window with difficulty, and I saw the street looking like a slim rivulet with cars oozing through. I pulled my head inside. I was too nervous. I did not understand what was going on. I put the desk supplies down on the floor, and lay back with my head on the desk and my feet dangling off from my knees.

How could I know how much time had passed when I fell from the desk and saw it as small as a stool? My head was shoved up against one wall and my feet against the opposite wall. My clothes were too small and tight. My shoes were squeezing my feet hard. I got up wondering, and my head hit the roof. I looked at the time and the date. Three hours had passed. Three hours and four days and six weeks. I could see the clock hands turning smoothly and quickly. I opened the door and left, all crumpled up. I was looking for the elevator when I saw the exit. I pushed myself through and got outside. I took a look at the building. It was one story high.

I walked in the street. The little cars were driving. When I was four, I had cars like them, and a second later they were the ones I used to pull behind me on a string.

I stepped over the cars, over to the other side of the street. I began to walk along it, next to the cars. There were no clothes on my body. I was entirely naked. The tallest man was maybe ten centimeters tall. The walls on either side of the street were closing in second by second, the buildings getting lower.

I stepped up on a building and looked around. I could see almost the whole city, and after a while the whole country. Everything was visible, like when you get far from the earth and see it as a turning globe. I saw it as a turning globe I was trundling it under my feet. It became so small its gravity could no longer hold me. I became suspended in space and left earth to itself. The stars and the galaxies were like pearls and sequins splashed on a dress. They were small – everything was small. I was in a cone, and I escaped from its larger mouth. There was nothing else. The cone became small, too small – I could not get back in anymore. It was small and golden, just like a little horn. I picked it up and examined it. I put my mouth to it and blew: "Beep!"

Dance Me to the End of Love

It has happened many times in my life that I have been kind to someone who did not deserve it, and have respected to someone who did not deserve it, and have paid attention to someone who did not deserve it. Once I paid attention to some resin. The resin was not in the city. It was living in a village, somewhere in a garden, on a tree. It was boorish. At first, it did not bat an eye when it noticed that I noticed it. It held tightly to the tree and looked aggressive.

There is someone in me that fools me. If I am not fooled by him, I cannot live my life. I might say all of my deeds have been done according to his deceptions, except most deeds are not like that. He fooled me in this case though, when I acknowledged the resin and it continued its apathetic, stupid life on the tree.

I touched it. It was an interesting feeling, because it has an interesting shape. The resin was like a semitransparent ball with a color similar to honey. A little dust had covered it. "What's that?" I asked my dad, and he answered "Resin," and I learned its name and decided to separate it from the tree. The pathetic floozy did not even resist – as it saw my hand coming to pull it off the tree, it just gave up and jumped right into my hand's hug. It was viscid, and like every viscid thing it went too far, and stuck to my fingers. Still, it was interesting to me, remained interesting… and then not interesting anymore. I soon become bored with interesting things.

It fell from grace, but my hand did not fall from grace along with it. I did not want to communicate with it at all, and I rubbed it off on a big sedimentary rock and got away. I was laughing in my heart when I heard the sound of laughter. I wondered about that, because the sound of laughter in my heart never comes out, except in special cases. The sound was from my hand, and I looked it with fear. A little resin was stuck on my palm and was annoying me like the strawberry odor of factory-produced cakes, and its laughter was something like that damned Leonard Cohen with his bullshit "Dance Me to the End of Love". I didn't even have anything to wipe it off with.

The resin lived on my hand for next few days. Even when I washed it, I saw a combination of annoyance and insistence gleaming in its eyes. There was no escape; the resin, like a responsible mother, had taken my hand and never let go. It had fallen in love with my hand. It was boorish, and it was impossible to get rid of it. I gave it my hand, and forgot the whole thing, and left it there on my hand forever.

At the Breakfast Table

In bygone days, there was a man who lived with three children and a wife. They used to do everything together. They used to eat breakfast together, they used to eat lunch together, they used to eat dinner together. They used to go out together, they used to come back in from out together. They used to laugh together, they used to stand up to-gether, they used to say hello together, they used to say goodbye together. They used to speak together, they used to get quiet and listen together, they used to watch tele-vision together, they used to listen to the radio together, they used to look at photos together. The man's three children were a boy, a girl, and another one who was neither a boy nor a girl. They were his wife's children too. His wife, herself, had given birth to all three. His son was thin and his daughter was fat and one was neither thin nor fat.

Once, when they were eating breakfast together, the man talked about butter. He did not talk about butter by himself, they all talked about butter together. Their talk went on for a while, but at last, the wife, the boy, and the girl and the one who was neither a girl nor a boy stopped talking. The man was still talking. The four remained silent and wondered. The man did not wonder, because he was still talking, and that's why they were wondering — it was the first time the man was doing something alone. The man was nitpicking something about the butter, so there was a lot to say. That was once.

The next time he nitpicked while looking at a landscape, and his wife and his three children gave up looking at the landscape, but wondered. The third time it was about his daughter's obesity. "Why did you get so fat?" he asked his daughter. "Because I ate a lot" she answered. But this answer was not enough for the man, so he nitpicked it.

The fourth time was when he said to his last child: "You aren't a boy." "It's obvious," it answered. The man said: "You aren't a girl either." "You know I'm not a girl," it answered. But the matter did not end there. The man nitpicked too much. Once again he nitpicked his son's weight loss and nitpicked the lunch his wife had made.

The man was nitpicking for a long time and he did not give up. His son got married in order to leave home. His daughter worked for herself as a travel agent so she could get away from her father. The one who was neither a boy nor a girl met out-of-the-ordinary people and left home forever. After that, his wife spent all her time going and coming to and from the court. She had decided to separate. The man was not ready to give up.

He nitpicked all the time while everything around him changed. They did not do anything together anymore. They ate breakfast alone, they ate lunch alone, they ate dinner alone. They went out alone, they came back in from out alone. They laughed alone, they stood up alone, they said hello alone, they said goodbye alone. They spoke alone, they became silent and listened alone, they watched television alone, they listened to the radio alone, they looked at photos alone.

This process continued, and the man loved the taste of nitpicking. He enjoyed it and felt good. Once he thought his hair was too long and inconvenient for nitpicking. So he went to a barber shop and his hair was cut, fell to the floor of the shop, and was gone. Thereafter he nitpicked with incomparable ease. He had become professional at his job. He could nitpick even alone. He could nitpick easily in the least possible space – like under the bed, or under the fridge, or even in the jewelry box. He did nothing else anymore. He did not eat. He did not converse. He did not take a bath. He did not look at landscapes. He did not even scratch if he itched. He did not think about anything. He did not sleep. He did not wake up. He did not acknowledge people walking on the sidewalk. He did not close the bathroom door if it was open and the smell was bad. He just nitpicked.

Years passed, and the man left the bygone days and arrived at now. He is just as the same as he was in those days, because he did not even spend time getting old. His ex-wife is dead. His son is a scrawny old man. His daughter is dying of obesity, but her grandchildren cannot get her to have surgery. The one who was neither a boy nor a girl had disappeared. Now the man is sitting and nitpicking without any resistance and at every opportunity. One time he sat down on a chair and is still sitting there preparing for historical and unparalleled nitpicking.

The Endless Stories

Our life is different from other people's. We have a grandmother in our family and someone who tells stories, but these two are not the same person. My grandmother never told a story to anyone, and has only sung songs and scraped together various poems. Sometimes others cook a lot of food, and she eats and grabs a corner to sleep in until she wakes up and asks, "What time is it?" That's because she is too young, and as a grandmother, she still needs more experience. Surely you understand that such a person does not tell stories. No stories.

We have a niece. My niece is many people's niece. She tells stories to all of them.

She knows many stories, in many languages, from many countries, from many religions, in many designs and colors. She is very old. She is older than everybody to whom she tells stories. Grandmother does not respect her. She does not even care about her age. Once my niece was telling a story for her hundreds of thousands of aunts and uncles that I want to tell you here:

Once upon a time, when everything came from God, at that time, in a warm season, on one of the good days, in one of the far-away towns, there was an old man living in a wooden cottage far from the city. One day, while he was cutting a tree trunk into pieces, he suddenly found that he had cut someone's head off his neck. There was a head and a neck of a little man buried in the trunk. His pus and blood were pouring out on the handle and caused the ax to fall from the old man's hand. "I killed him" the old man told himself. The little man's corpse was swelling every moment and becoming bigger. It became so huge that the old man ran to the cottage horrified. The swollen corpse followed him. The old man picked up the hunting rifle from the wall and tried to load it, but since his hands were shaking, he could not do it right. The corpse was forcing its entry through the small door-frame of the cottage. The old man was shivering head to toe. The cartridge fell from his hand. As he tried to bend and pick it up, Grandmother said "That's enough!" "What?" our niece asked. "Tell the ending or don't tell the story at all. It's boring," Grandmother said. "I won't tell it at all then. That's how it happened," our niece said. The aunts and the uncles got upset. Grandmother was pleased and said, "So I'll sing a poem". Then she started to sing some poem by Baraheni, but nobody liked it. Then she sang some tune by the Jonas brothers, but nobody enjoyed that either. Grandmother couldn't keep down her youthful excitement, so she played tracks of some very fancy songs on a CD player and danced a lot, but finally nobody liked it. This is how things always go, and my niece's stories remain endless. I will tell some of her other endless stories later. The aunts and the uncles went and made plans for more recent events.

The Other

When they saw the light, they were frightened, but they did not lose their heads over that. In fact, they had no actual heads to lose. They hid themselves among the villi and began to imitate them. The light became stronger, meaning the source was getting closer and closer. They bent the way the villi bent, waving and dancing to the villi's tune. They had to be careful; they were so much bigger than the villi, bigger and fatter. But all three did so well that they themselves believed their movements were just like the villi's. An extremely bright light shone into their faces but they did not even blink. They did not want to attract attention. The light source had entered. It was like them, like a worm but certainly much longer, with one single eye and a very shiny light on its head.

It had entered the stomach from the end of the esophagus, pushed on to the duodenum, and was turning its head side to side. The rest of its body was still in the stomach and esophagus. It was obviously very long, and had come from somewhere none of the three could imagine. That such a creature might arrive and turns its head around meant nothing to them. But they themselves – like those who know they are doing evil – reacted to everything by hiding.

Suddenly the stomach began to sway and shake. The villi were ok with the shaking, because they were off in the duodenum. But the three of them didn't feel comfortable with that intense shaking because they were not villi. They were only three little worms that had seen nothing except the duodenum with dark spaces above and below, with edibles coming from one and going into the other. Such intense shaking almost upended them to air their dirty linen in public. Since all three had the same instinct – like people who coordinate their minds via telepathy – they understood that a wandering endoscope was causing the intense shaking, and they turned quickly flipped over, and grabbed onto the duodenal crust with their tiny teeth. They all laughed at the endoscope, for no matter how much it shook, it could not shake them free. With that thought, they became more determined and clamped down even harder with their teeth. The duodenum shook violently. The endoscope turned its head and shone its light on all the villi. At that moment, one of the worms, stimulated by the delicious taste of the duodenal crust, and excited by the sharp smell of the increased stomach acid, could tolerate no more. Regardless of the last time food had flushed from the esophagus into the stomach, it had been a long time since something had entered the duodenum and intestinal tract. So it began to chew. The duodenum shook more fiercely than ever. The worm who had bitten its crust took a little more away in its teeth. The duodenum shook again. And suddenly the worm felt brightness all around. The light was shining directly on it, and though it could not see, it felt the heavy look of the stranger. It froze in its tracks.

On the other side, the two in darkness raised their heads and looked over to where the stranger's light was shining directly on the lonely worm. They moved together slowly, up toward the point where the endoscope had come from the stomach. They slipped carefully and smoothly among the villi and were impossible to see. The endoscope checked around to make sure the worm had no accomplices, then began receding. The pair were holding themselves together with great difficulty, because they were not used to it. They tried not to move, and hoped the stranger would leave soon.

The endoscope was pulling slowly back into the stomach and esophagus. When the exposed worm saw the light withdrawing and darkness returning, it again felt relieved, and began chewing at the duodenum before the endoscope was completely out. The duodenum became frenetic and twisted around. The other two worms could not hold on. They released their jaws and when the endoscope left, they fell down into the intestine. While falling, they pecked out continually, but there was nothing to bite and hold on to as they were thrown straight into the intestine. It was not clear how far.

The first worm was still chewing the duodenal crust and was unconcerned with the heavy shaking. It never thought about what had happened to the other two. Though they never were friends, and each had its own life, it possibly might feel a little afraid if left completely alone. But there was another possibility: perhaps it was entirely unaware of the others. Maybe they had never seen each other in the darkness, and it was only instinct that had synchronized them. Maybe under the endoscopic light, it was the first time they had been aware of one another's existence.

Some moments passed. There was no food coming down, and the worm continued to eat the duodenum. Suddenly a strange, delicate odor from the stomach filled the duodenal space, a good smell that intoxicated the worm and stopped its gnawing. It followed the smell, slipped smoothly among the villi, and continued until it got to the stomach, its whole body immersed in a thick liquid that smelled better than stomach acid. It began to drink that fragrant liquid, and found it more delicious than the duodenal crust. The meal made it dizzy. It had never been so anxious to eat anything else. It was eating, unaware of becoming lethargic, so languid and feeble that eating became unconscious, a feeding with no more will. The liquid was filling its body and replacing its spirit. The little worm - while dying - was slowly inflating and growing.

The two other worms had not fallen too far into the intestine and they quickly returned. The corpse of the dead worm was growing second by second. Suddenly, it exploded, and everything it had drunk up in the stomach released its delicate odor. The smell speeded up the pair. The thick liquid was flowing toward them and its fragrance was driving them crazy. And then the stomach and the duodenum were calmer than they had ever been before.

The worm that arrived soonest began to eat, occasionally ingesting parts of the dead worm and becoming dizzy. The second arrived only when the first had eaten too much and almost died, inflated and huge. It had not yet eaten anything when suddenly it heard a sound from the esophagus and before it understood what was happening, was hit by a flood of dilute liquid, washing everything toward the intestine. The last worm alive remained, bracing itself at the intestinal opening.

A doctor entered the room with a paper in his hand, and the patient, with spent expectation in his eyes, followed the doctor to the desk. The doctor looked at his pale face and slim body and said: "You feel better, don't you?". The man nodded his head. "Fine. The medication worked. There were bodies of two little worms in your test sample," the doctor said. It was obvious by the patient's unhappy look that the doctor's words had not pleased him. The doctor continued: "There was a little worm seen in the endoscopy too. Do you feel any pain?" The man nodded. "That's from the small wounds. You'll get better." The patient had a question in his eyes that the doctor tried to answer: "If you don't feel better come back next week." The patient knew his words would be useless, so he got up before the last sentence, went toward the door - and without looking back - opened the door and left.

The worm had not been afraid of the light. It did not even try to hide. It had been chewing the duodenal crust and did not care about all the intestinal shaking and waving when the endoscope entered. It had not found that strange. It was just some giant worm with a single eye and a very shiny light on its head. When it began to squirm and twist from side to side, the worm had carefully watched its behavior from the intestinal opening. Through the endoscope's movements and under its dancing light, the worm had seen something interesting: in every part of the duodenum it had shown on, he had seen worms his own size, a little smaller or a little bigger. Some were trying to hide among the villi, but their cohort had been able to see them too.

Collaboration! It was the first time such a thought had occurred to the worm's small brain. In the darkness, it did not know how long it was those many worms had been there feeding. They had never been friends.

They each had their own lives, and none of them hiding among the villi had been aware of anyone else's existence. The endoscope light shone directly on the worm. The worm looked at the light. It had been hard on its eyes, but after some blinking, it was able to keep its eyes open. With open eyes, it had begun chewing on the villi, while enjoying the smell of acid, the light, and the intense shaking of the stomach and duodenum.

To Be Thrown by the Light

It hadn't moved from there, somewhere in the world, in a small room, under the carpet. It was a secret. A secret between two people, and they had gone. They had gone and never come back. Years had passed. It was still under the carpet. On a small rectangular piece of paper. That rectangle wasn't its home. Its home was between those two people or in that "between-two-people" space. For anything not a secret, it is hard to imagine; living between two people is not good at all. Because this between is not somewhere like a small village or an apartment, or the shell of a snail. It is somewhere that has no resemblance with any place to live.

The only thing which makes a secret alive is hope. Many people who are not secrets are alive like this too, but this hope is quite different. The poor secret under the carpet was alive with only the hope of being someday revealed. Being revealed is so interesting. It's like being killed for a big goal. The secret was alive hoping to be killed. Many years had passed and the secret was still on the small rectangle, in that snapshot of memento, between the two people in the photo whose whereabouts are currently unknown.

One could hope that on a scary night, a wind might suddenly break through the window, and move the carpet, and make the photo fly in the room. And once the sky thunders, if a neighbor were out front, looking in the window, he would see a photo floating in the room. And if the neighbor became curious, and took steps to make sure nobody was home, and jumped over the wall, if anything impeded his steps, he wouldn't be afraid and decide not to continue. He would finally enter the room, and if the photo were in an obvious place, and he picked it up and took a look at it, and if he recognized the two in the picture. He would be shocked.

The neighbor would tell everything to everybody and the secret would be revealed as it truly deserves. But things are not that hopeful. Because it is probable that when the neighbor came up against a barrier he would crumble. It is even possible that he would never have become curious. It might happen that there would be no neighbor there. Maybe there would have been no wind that scary night, and maybe the room would have had no window.

Anyway, the secret was still under the carpet and it was not very conscious of the things going on around. Alas! Consciousness! It was expecting someday to fall into the fire of consciousness, and to vanish as it was being revealed. Then a question came into its mind: "Why didn't it know much about its surroundings?" The secret had not always been under the carpet! It was wondering where it had been before. It pondered this, but remembered nothing but the moment of being projected on the photographic paper. Nothing else did it remember! It became anxious. Did that mean it was facing oblivion? It thought that might not be true. If I am oblivious why am I remembering that moment? Then it wondered more reasonably, and thought that if it was remembering that moment, it is because of that tiny rectangle, the photo which was under the carpet along with it. It thought much and remembered nothing but the photo and the carpet. It became even more anxious. Believing that it had really become oblivious, just like a poison, made it numb from head to toe. It didn't know anything. It told itself…

Suddenly the carpet moved, and a painful light shone on the photo. There in the room were a middle-aged man and woman. The woman was standing, and the man sitting, and the man's hand was holding up one corner of the carpet. The woman bent down and picked up the photo. She looked at the photo, without any special feeling in her eyes; the photo was of a young girl and boy. The woman stood next to the man and showed him the photo. The man examined it, then he threw it on the floor. He stared at the woman and the woman stared at him. There was something between them that had no shape. The woman and the man both felt its presence. The man asked: "Who are you?" It answered: "I don't know. I don't remember anything." The man said: "There used to be a secret here, have you seen it?" It answered, "I don't remember anything." The man said: "We came to get our secret so as to reveal it. But it seems it's not there." It answered: "I have forgotten everything."

The woman left the room without caring about their conversation. The man saw her leaving, and he too left. The room became empty again.

Alteration

He should just find some private place, a place where he couldn't be seen. He knew where there was such a place. Without doubt he'd go there. He didn't review anything in his mind – not any sweet memory or long-standing sorrow. He had completely forgotten everyone he loved, and didn't think about his enemies. Neither sorrow nor fear. Neither happy nor thoughtful. He knew exactly what he should do; it was so simple, so simple that he didn't think about what might come.

Just here. He'd arrived at the place he was looking for – four walls, high, wide, surrounding an empty yard, behind the remains of an old factory. He unfurled a coil of rope attached to a grappling hook. After one or two spins, he hurled the hook up toward the top of the wall. It hit the wall and bounced back at him. He jumped away to avoid it. Then he paused for a moment, thought about what he was doing, and laughed. He laughed – laughed about his concern that something might be dangerous. He threw the hook again. He was more careful this time, and so the hook that depended on his accuracy suspended itself for a second over the fence at the top of the wall, and then fell on one of its bars and caught there. He pulled on the rope until he felt sure it was tight. Then he grabbed the rope with his hands, pushed against the wall with his feet, and took confident, small steps, climbing slowly. All of a sudden, his foot slipped and his heart sped up, beating hard under his ribs. He laughed again – this was the second time he was afraid of danger, even while walking voluntarily, in full knowledge, into danger. He reached the fence and held the bars in his hands. He breathed deeply, but uncomfortably, anxious about passing from one level to another. He looked over to the other side of the wall; it was more extensive than he had thought, and it was not the pristine, private place he had fantasized. At the base of the wall – all around it – the dirt was stacked and hardened. In places the color had been changed by chemical waste. The chassis of a wrecked LaSalle glowed near the west wall. Though it had no tires and was so rusted that it was impossible to tell from the remnants of paint whether its color had been blue or white, it still looked like it was running hot, and the heavy warm sound of its engine still remained in its flesh.

There was nothing any more interesting. Everything scattered all round looked raw and useless and crude; in the bevy of things were forms and I-beams and flat bars and rebar piled one on another and mixed together, piece by piece, useless and rusty. Although they were certainly more useful than that old junk car, it was that that stood out as the most impressive – its existence made him think that perhaps there were better things down there. He laughed again, stuck in his normal life, unable to think about his mission. That's where he wanted to be. He didn't want anyone to find him, his body, yelling and screaming. He didn't want his suicide to be on the news, with everyone trying to guess the reason for his act. His ideal state was possible here. He thought nobody would be aware if he died within these four walls, and at worst, people would come only when worms and insects had left behind nothing of his flesh. First, he wanted to be fully naked, to burn all his clothes so his body might be available for living creatures to fatten up on his corpse, leaving no trace. All this was in his mind while he was still up on the wall. Initially he thought he should stand up completely so he could step over the fence, go over to the other side, and climb down with the rope. He thought that way because he was holding onto the bars with bent legs, inspecting the wreckage, and imagining what was to come.

But standing that high up was not simple, especially with his longstanding vertigo just waiting for some height to whirl around in his head. He stood up with great difficulty. He raised his left foot, but couldn't balance. So he turned in that narrow space with such excitement and accuracy that it made his hands tremble a little until he could raise his right foot. It was simpler that way. His right foot made it over to the other side of the bars. The left foot is always problematic. The right foot was on the wall on the other side, and the left one on this side was hanging above it. He inched his foot over until that less flexible one finally joined its partner. But turned around, pressed against the bar, his balls were in terrible trouble. His vertigo found the best opportunity to satisfy its last desire, collaborated with the pain and fell off the wall, not to the ground, but onto that pile of countless useless things – onto the I-beams and rebar and forms. He fell on them hard, and a rebar ripped right under his chin, right through to his palate, and his kneecap was crushed by a long narrow I-beam, and now hung bloodily outside his knee.

It was impossible for him to shout, and even the least movement was difficult. He was completely alive, feeling pain with every dutiful nerve. All those zigzag iron hands, like his on-going supporters, were holding him close. If they were able to shout like those supporters, maybe there would be hope for somebody to know he was here. But no – who could pass by?

His blood was gradually leaving him. He hoped to pass out soon to be rid of the pain. He wondered vaguely if his own planned method would have worked more quickly than what was happening now. And would that have been a suicide at all? His dying accidently – and not as the deliberate deed he'd wanted and decided on – tortured his soul more than the pain in his body. He remembered everything at that moment – all the forgotten memories he didn't want to remember.

First, he thought of yesterday, when he saw his high school classmate and pretended not to know him. The poor classmate tried so hard to remind him, but he, who didn't want to remember, was stronger. He didn't know why, but now he wanted that classmate to be there with him. He couldn't figure out if the nostalgia he felt for a person he had met yesterday after many years represented some kind of despair about his firm decision to commit suicide.

He saw the LaSalle out of the corner of his eye. The vision was incomplete, as if the car itself was there without his being able to see it. He thought it might be more promising for him if he could have fallen in a day when the driver was still in the LaSalle, instead of today. Maybe his brain was not working right from loss of blood; what could the driver of the LaSalle be doing in that courtyard? Such a thought smelled sick. He thought of television. He didn't know why, but the memory of television took over his mind for a while. He had been going to repair his television set. For a long time, it had been impossible to turn down the volume, and the TV was shouting all the time. It was just two weeks before his decision that he had asked his neighbor where he could get the set repaired. He knew exactly how to get to the repair shop if he could get out of that courtyard. How he now wanted the repair man to know he would appreciate it if his TV could work well!

Everything was slowly changing. He was thinking, too, that he had never been wise, never. He had never realized how enjoyable turning the key in the front door was.

He had never recognized how interesting it was to hold your hand under the cold water and wait for it to get warm. And because of the rusted steel spike, he could now understand the enjoyment of the broken bedspring when it pressed into his back. He was now sure that he had been a superficial, thoughtless person, and was himself more miserable than anyone he had thought to humble or play around with. He was now sure that he had been drab and inert all his life – just as he was now – and that he had always had these walls around him, four high walls that let no one see or know him.

At that moment, a quiet sound of music suddenly hummed in his ear, a very faint sound, that grew into an earsplitting pop song. He got excited. His heart beat faster, making him bleed faster, but because of excitement and tension he no longer felt sluggish. He did not know how much time had passed since his fall or how long it had been since the rebar had pinned his tongue to his palate. But now, with the rhythm of that song ringing in his ears, he was feeling every single second, and even tinier time units – one would say every hundred thousandth of a second – more massively, and holding on for eternity. The volume of the song increased and decreased like the irritation of two deep wounds. He was wishing the rebar and I-beam had both plunged more deeply so he could at least touch the ground and pull them out of his body. But losing so much blood, his brain could not work right, or he would have understood that any further penetration would have split his skull and killed him instantly. But in that situation – being suspended without being able to push on anything with any part of his body – it was the only wish he could have. In fact, a sudden death would have been better for him, but his skull was too hard to be pierced by rusted rebar.

The sound didn't stop, and remained unchanged. The sound he was hearing could not exist – that repetitious song. Where could it be from? He understood correctly that there was no actual song. His ears had taken over, and were hearing without his will, and independently of the outside world, and only because of a brain malfunction. An excited rush came again, but not one of happiness and hope. He recognized now that his time had come, a fact that made him nervous. No doubt, he had to laugh at himself once more. He had come here to finish things off, but now finishing off was scaring him. If he were not in this situation – despite the fear – he would certainly have run miles away. What from and where to? He didn't know.

He didn't know what was going on – but what was going on was simple: blood loss and extreme fatigue was making him lethargic. This was what he had been waiting for, but now he was afraid of his anesthesia. "What if this is not just anesthesia? Maybe I'm going to die". That was what was in his mind. Just like people who have never parachuted off a plane. They would like to make the big leap. They think about it fondly, and see it in their dreams, and finally one day they will actually try do-ing it. They get on a plane and look down from the height. The plane is still climbing and they strap on their parachute, still sure about their decision. But when they stand at the door, and they have to jump out to where even giant buildings don't make the least impression, then they feel they were wrong. They can't do it. But momentum holds them by the neck and won't let go. Everything is prepared for their jump. If they hold back, someone will push them. He was now in the same situation. He remembered his university days when classmates tried to get close to him and he treated them like his dripping nose. He remembered the first day, during introductions, he refused to join in, and went to the men's room to be alone. He remembered registration day and the decisions he had to make to register in stupid classes all the students hated. He remembered when he calmly went to the registrar's office, arrogantly called the staff by their first names written on the name-plates at their desks, and announced that he wanted to quit. He couldn't tolerate even a semester. There, it was simple to quit. But here he was the only authority. He should to do something for himself if he was going to quit, but he was weaker than his dripping nasal mucosa. He imagined that if someone now showed up on top of the wall – some-one who also wanted to commit suicide- he too would focus on the LaSalle. Even that old rusted iron box was more interesting than he was. He held his eyes open with all his might to keep himself from drifting off. But as death comes, eyelids bow before it and close over eyes, just as was happening. The eyes under his lids didn't move side to side as they did when he was asleep.

How long had it been? Not clear at all.

But however many minutes it was, he was nobody anymore – only a mass of meat and bones on two skewers, suspended between the air and the earth. The blood that had poured from his wounds had changed the color of the soil as did those chemical wastes. Muscles had stopped controlling and commanding, and urine, once locked in a bladder, came out freely, passed through his pants and rained down beside the clotted blood. His nose had given up on olfaction and the smell of the urine that had foamed on the soil had no effect anymore. Intestines wouldn't be so limp if there was still life in them, but now thin and watery stool was free to glide down his trouser leg and pour out on the orange, rusted iron. This expanded mass could never have imagined that these stinking red, yellow and brown patterns would be there at its death. The flies soon arrived, indifferent to whether they landed on iron, on meat, or on stool. They just sat and sucked, and rose and spawned for the duration. They laid tiny larvae on every part of the corpse – on eyelids, on lips, in nostrils, in ears, between the fine hairs on the face and on the back of the neck. Everywhere were infants that would soon begin to move and be fed from that rich mass.

Nothing was treading the footprints of time but dimming light, blowing wind, and the movement of flies and ants. Time was passing unmarked, however it wished, and the tiny larvae, now little worms, were feasting on all they could eat. Now there were no eyelids closed over eyeballs, and the eyeballs themselves were gone. The tongue, once pinned to the palate by rebar, was gone. The urine had evaporated, and only the soil, pock-marked and stiff, remained. The blood was dark and clotted, and the remaining stool had dried on iron.

The wreckage looked different. The La-Salle seemed ashamed in the presence of such corruption – as if that rusted iron frame could not tolerate such an obscenely boring image, an image that grew more disgusting as time passed. The shape of the once-living creature who had fallen down the wall had been transformed by hundreds of thousands of worms living brutally, eating greedily, like lustful dogs gnawing at the back of a woman, all of them growing to become mothers who would someday leave their own larvae. All these had altered everything, and the blessed result was that no living creature would have anything to do with the remaining bones.

Some days or months later, the lonely LaSalle's wishes were fulfilled. A long crane arm appeared from the southern wall – the wall which had been squeezing his balls with the horizontal bars atop its fence, and conspired there with a hot-blooded vertigo. A thick arm loaded with scraps on its magnetic hand dropped them on the bones more fragile than an sensational suicide.

To Lick

The little girl lost her balloon, and walked through the park to the other side. The balloon flew up and after a while saw the little girl buying another one. It tried to land again, but couldn't. It was not at all clear to it that the little girl had meant to let it go. It exhaled with all its might but that did nothing because it was not its breath that raised it up, it was the gas injected into its body.

As it got higher, the air around was getting colder and windy, and the little girl and the people in the park were getting smaller, and the other balloons were getting tinier and more insignificant. The little girl looked up and saw her balloon flying fearlessly up. But the balloon was so far away that it couldn't see the little girl watching. It never understood why the little girl had left it alone. The new balloon was swinging randomly on a plastic stick in the little girl's hand.

The little girl was excited by the escape of her previous balloon, so she decided to watch new balloon fly up too. She released it, but the new balloon couldn't fly. She threw it up in the air, but it didn't climb. The little girl didn't like being watched by all the other people, and that's why she left the new balloon alone and went away. But nobody had really noticed the little girl. It was only her imagination that everybody was watching her. The new balloon fell to the ground, rolled aimlessly a few times, and then tried to stand up tall, but couldn't. It never understood why the little girl had left it alone.

A clean-shaven man poked his car key into the new balloon's cheek. The new balloon was watching the little girl buying yet another balloon. The pressure of the key grew until it could not see anything anymore and exploded. Its lifeless parts were blown everywhere with tremendous speed. The first balloon was still flying in the sky. The little girl bought a very deluxe balloon she felt she could count on. She released it for a second and the deluxe balloon started going up. She grabbed the stick fast.

She was so happy she went to look for other kids so they could see the moment her balloon took off. She released the deluxe balloon, but other kids weren't watching. It went up, swinging left and right in the hands of the wind until it hit a tree branch. It was dying of fear at that moment, but it tried to stay clear-headed, because it knew that this was its last moment of life. Then, it exploded, and left its pieces hanging on the branches and the leaves. Even the little girl didn't see the explosion because she had gone to buy an even bigger balloon that stood out among the others and had no match. She wondered why she hadn't bought that one first. She bought the huge balloon and hugged it. It could not fit in the little girl's arms, but it enjoyed the hug; the little girl's arms felt good.

The huge balloon found the squeaks of its thick skin most interesting. But the little girl didn't notice the sound, and was proud only of its size. Its stick dragged on the ground as she walked. The little girl turned around and considered the plastic stick. In her opinion, it was absolutely useless. She pulled it hard until it detached from the balloon. The huge balloon could not figure out what was going on; pulling out the stick hurt a lot. It had felt pain like that only after its prostate surgery. But this was much more serious. It hurt badly until the stick came out, and that was the end of the story. The big balloon felt nothing anymore, because it had stopped existing. In separating from the stick, it had exploded, and now its soul was ascending lightly and freely, flying so fast. It saw the little girl throwing the stick away and walking toward the balloon man. Flying up, everything became so small. Suddenly it saw a balloon nearby. It was the first balloon, still flying. The huge balloon soul tried to make friends, but that first balloon exploded from the drop in pressure. The huge balloon was surprised, and realized an important thing; it was the only balloon who had had a soul in addition to its body. The little girl was going to buy a thin balloon that was long and a million miles from beautiful. But there was not much money left, and with that money she could only buy a lollipop. That's why she bought a large flat spiral lollipop and began to lick.

The Small Metal Scissors

He was in the car. In the darkness of the night, he noticed something glinting on the shoulder of the road. Stopped. Switched the car off. Lowered the passenger side window. Frowned and looked carefully. While he was looking, he did nothing else. It was an intense gaze. As if he had to gaze like that from then on, all his life, on the same road, on the same night. But it was not like that. He rolled up the passenger side window, and turned the key. The car coughed and turned on. Moved.

He turned the car stereo on, and did not mind the song. As if the stereo had turned on by itself. No one was singing. Some

band was playing. He could hear every in-
strument except those that were not there.
Tiny fluorescent blips like short-lived stars
flashed for a while and then were gone. He
was not watching them because he was
looking ahead. Unless they came into view.

He scratched the outside corner of his
eye. He scratched the outside corner of his
eye a second time. He scratched the outside
corner of an eye a third time. He squinted,
annoyed by the lights of a car behind him.
He slowed down, and moved over to the
right. The car behind did not pass. Click,
click – he turned the left turn light on and
off. Still, the car behind did not pass. He
slowed down a bit more, rolled down his
window and held his arm out, waving the
car on to pass. The car behind did not pass,
but turned its flashers on. He brought his
arm back inside, drove the car over to the
shoulder, and stopped. The car behind
pulled over, a few meters back.

Both drivers got out. He scratched the

corner of his eye, and walked toward the car in back. Its driver, a stranger, walking faster, approached him and said, "Hi, excuse me…" he answered "Hi, what's going on?" "Excuse me for flashing! Apologies!" the stranger said. "What's up?" he asked. "We're running out of gas," the stranger answered, pointing to his car. Two or three persons were sitting in the darkness of the car. "Can we get some gas from your car?" the stranger asked. "I have no hose. Do you have one?" he asked. "I don't… can I get the gas from the carburetor?" the stranger asked. "Only from the tank… was that you?" he asked. "We?… When?" the stranger asked. "A little way back along the road I saw something… Wasn't that you?" he asked. "Something? What? Was it a car?" the stranger asked. "Don't know, didn't understand, it was dark and it looked like…" the stranger pointed over to the side and asked "Like that?" He scratched the corner of his eye and looked. Looked intently. As if he had to look forever.

He gazed wonderingly and answered, "Yes, I think so…!" and walked toward his car. He turned his head back for a second, and saw the stranger open the door of his car; the passengers were lit up. He turned away and quickly got into his own car and started it up. In the mirror he saw the stranger coming toward him carrying a plastic gas can. But he did not wait and left.

He scratched the corner of his eye. Driving away. Driving away. Driving away continuously. The eye did not leave him alone. He stopped. Turned on the light above the mirror. Faced the mirror. Looked at himself. His eyebrow was long and bent and a hair had gotten into the corner of his eye. He opened the glove compartment. It was interesting to open the glove compartment because he had done that before. He had done it, and had looked for something. He was looking for something. Got out of the car and went to the trunk. Opened it. It was interesting to open the trunk because he had done that before. Because he had been looking for something. Rummaged around. Opened a small metal box and it was interesting to open that too. It was full of small metal things. He scratched the corner of his eye. He slammed the trunk. It did not close. Slammed again, it did not close. He paused for a few seconds, lowered the trunk lid slowly and pushed down once. Closed.

He got back inside and looked in the mirror. He pulled at his eyebrow. Could not be plucked. He pulled. The skin was stretching and moving on his forehead, but the eyebrow still was there. He scratched the corner of his eye. He tried to re-shape the eyebrow tail with his fingers, but the eyebrow hair insisted on moving back into the corner of his eye. All that was interesting. He had done it all before.

He started the car. Stepped on the gas and turned the wheel. Went over to the other side into the opposite lane. He was going back. Going back, with gas. Going back, still going back. On the other side, he saw what he had seen before on the shoulder. But no, it was the thing the stranger had shown him. Apparently, the stranger had found gas and left. It was interesting, because they had found gas and left before. Perhaps they never left.

He still was going. Going. Now he saw the thing. He turned the wheel completely, went over around to the previous lane and stopped beside the thing. He got out. Got close to it. It was absolutely dark. It was a car. It was entirely burnt, most of it smashed and hard to see. But its trunk lid was open and smiling. He looked and smiled back at the trunk lid. He got closer and opened it wide. Rummaged around. Opened the small metal box. It was full of small metal things. Rummaged around and found the scissors. The scissors opened in his hand and smiled. He smiled too. He found the eyebrow tail with his fingers, held it, pulled it, and put it in the scissors' mouth. It was as long as his other eyebrow. He paused. Scratched the corner of his eye once more.

A trailer was coming up behind him. It was getting close, swerving on the road, boozy and staggering. The scissors had still not finished its job, because he still was scratching the corner of his eye. He turned his head. He saw the trailer getting close. It was interesting. He had seen it getting close before. He frowned and looked carefully. Suddenly his eyes opened wide. He was still looking. As if he had to gaze at this road and this night, forever.

Live

So you know? He was so creative. Of course, he didn't take baths and he picked his nose at lunch. But I don't at all want to relate such issues to his creativity, because those things are indeed bad. You shouldn't ask me about his behavior in our congenial space, because I'm saying things that are not related to his artistic and innovative life, and they may cause misinterpretation and get out to people somehow. For instance, when he used a toothpick, he pulled out particles of food from his teeth and flicked them onto the mirror. There were always many particles sticking to the mirror, it was hard to clean them, and it took a lot of time.

Is that good? Of course not! What else do you want to know? That he left behind so many wonderful works is clear to everyone. He still does interesting things, although he has become an unbearable old man and even his wife has left him. Everybody knows he is a world-class artist, someone who knows what should be done because it's vital; he knows what he is doing, and he's also a prophet of ideas. Do you know what I'm talking about? It's as if ideas and plots emerge from somewhere into his mind. Even when executing them, he's just the same. It's impossible to find any technical problems. As I said before, he knows his work. Amazing.

But none of these things can justify his behavior. In all the time I knew him, he had no relationships with any girl, and that doesn't mean he was homosexual. He had problems with boys too. He had problems with everybody. In all those years I've never heard him say anything positive about anyone or about missing someone. He admired only great works of film and music and grumbled about everybody around him. But to be honest, I do have to say that he had one friend, one very close friend. You might suppose it was because they were similar, but that's not true, not at all. His friend was a perfectly friendly person. He had so many friends and was famous for being friendly. He would compromise with anybody and respected everyone. Perhaps this was the reason he could survive, although it was difficult for me to imagine any intimacy with him.

When he went out, he went alone. I used to think he was upset by his loneliness as a child because nobody would ever pick him up. That's why I once wanted to go out with him – but he didn't accept. I even insisted but he wouldn't agree. Afterwards, when I became closer to him, I very much regretted wanting to, and I cursed myself for done so.

There was nothing loveable from his point of view. His religious thoughts were his only objects of respect. It's hard to believe, but he used to pray in his dirty clothes, and his unbathed body violated religious principles. I have religious thoughts too, and I wondered about his behavior. I hope you don't censor anything when you're translating my words.

He knew everything. He knew about everything the news. That was his good side. He never ignored any discussion; whatever you were talking about, he could discuss it with you and stay with it till the end. If it was an argument, he could never lose. And even if that happened, he wouldn't give up. You couldn't figure out where his information come from. He used to stay in his room for days and days, come out only for toilet and food, and then, like a cockroach scared of light, he would run back there to his room. If he hated something, he'd criticize it enough to drive you crazy. In that case you should pretend to agree, otherwise the story would never end. But if he liked something, you should run away from him immediately – excuse me! My lips are chapped, so I can't laugh easily – anyway he was that kind of a person. I'd never seen anyone like him.

Now that I'm talking about him to you, you surely think that after several years of friendship I know him well. But I myself conclude – after the things I mentioned – that I don't know him at all. We're only close together, like a table and chair can be close together for years but nothing happens between them unless somebody comes and sits on the chair and eats on the table, or writes something, like maybe his friend. His good friend who never succeeded in being a famous artist. Of course, he didn't want to be, and he always used to say that it was just a coincidence he chose art as a major.

Anyway, you can't expect to know him from what I'm telling you. You'll publish this, and people will think they know many things about him. But while all this is the result of living by his side for several years, you can see it's very little, very little! I dare say I don't know anything more about him! Nothing. I don't know him at all!

The Hunter and the Hunted

The Hunter

Nothing could move the stone from its place. And who could say she was not a stone? What else could she be? She had built herself according to her self-image. She believed none of her organs could move at all, except for her fine hair. The wind was making it dance, and her heavy belly was filling and emptying with air passing through her nose and mouth with a regularity like the rising and sinking of the sun. Nothing could disturb the lioness's stillness, not even fury, a fury which was there, but there as quietly as if it were not, a fury which was hidden inside her gaze and flowing in her eyes like water under thin ice, releasing its poisonous arrow, and consuming her instinctive stalking of the tall gazelle.

An old male, with his big head and heavy sides, was lying under the shadow of the tree, rivaling its huge dry trunk in silence and stillness. The lioness was as motionless as he, but the way a time bomb is, a few seconds before explosion. She too was old. But who could make her believe that? She could still fill her stomach by herself, and would not easily surrender her body to the peace of death.

Nothing was hidden from her eyes, yet she was hidden from everyone else's. Not even the male could see her among the yellow grasses, and even the sun did not know that its fire raining on the grassland had a mass of gunpowder under its wide wings, lost in grassy wings of wavy yellows.

The gazelle came on so smoothly, it was impossible to tell if she were moving or not. All the old lioness's nerves were on edge, but she trembled not at all. She was waiting for the moment when she could see the gazelle's muscles twitching under its thin skin. She was waiting for the spark to explode her fury and burn crazily through her, head to toe. There was still a little time left. Only a little.

In an instant, her claws released from the ground. She could not remember the time when she was like a dead stone. The gazelle was still unaware of the sharp knives running toward it in the old lioness' half-open mouth. And a little above it, in the yellow staring eyes, an image of its torn-apart body was forming, painting blood-red the lips and teeth of two gigantic lions. But as if it saw all this, everything in the thin space between a before and an after just as thin, the gazelle's sharp slim legs decided to run sooner than did its small brain. The lioness was getting closer to the gazelle and the gazelle was getting farther away. Both were empty of everything; running was the only thing they were. If they did not run, they did not exist. The lioness was running away from a huge suffering, exactly as far from the suffering as she was close to the gazelle. She had to claw those twitching muscles to know that senility had not yet squeezed her dry.

Suddenly, the gazelle changed direction. The lioness followed it without the slightest hitch. Everything was arranged in her mind. Before hunting, she had planned exactly. The hunted was young and light; the hunter was heavy and old. The hunted was agile but unskilled; the hunter was more massive, but expert. They were still at a distance from one another. The gazelle did nothing the lioness did not know already; running this way, the lioness was following, running that way, the lioness was attacking from behind. It was as if a prisoner had a heavy ball and chain on his leg and however hard he pulled, his feet would drag the ball toward him. The gazelle was using all its energy to run, running faster and faster, second by second. But the lioness was running at the same speed she had started; not less, and not more. Steadily running, she was behind, while the gazelle was running with all its might, pouring its remaining force behind it like earth from a torn sack. At last the sack was empty, and the gazelle was dazedly hammering its hooves on the ground without knowing if it was going forward or not. Hammering hooves; hammering, and it still did not realize the searing pain was from the wound made by a furry old female's claws connecting her razor-sharp nails with her power.

The gazelle's legs bent and hit the ground and its muzzle hit the forest of sickle-like long grasses. Now it was feeling the weight of a lion it had always eluded. And it knew her steel fangs as well, because they were closer than its larynx. Both could hear the blood bubbling in the gazelle's throat - accompanying its last fruitless breaths. With its black eyes getting darker each second, it could not see the terrible visage, or the eyes streaming unbounded fury. And thereafter, only the lion and the grass and the sun saw what was happening to the now oily, slippery hunted.

The lioness returned to her defeated mate with a head weighed down by the gazelle's body. The old male slowly left his tree and approached his mate. The lioness was galloping toward him victorious, intoxicated with the pleasant odor of blood. Yes, galloping. Those slow steps she was taking, were as glorious as galloping. As they ate together, they performed a kind of sweet love-making without even touching, together tearing the sinews and muscles of the warm fresh kill. Nobody could see them except for the hungry, envious hyenas rising up a few at a time. Where were they until then? From what hole or hideout did the smell of blood and warm flesh attract them? They approached slowly with wary, conservative steps, stopping some distance from the lions, and sitting down to watch. The lioness saw them but paid no attention, amused at their thinking they could have any part of the spoils. She held each bloody scrap of flesh between her teeth, and chewed it with pride – a pride different from that of her mate. As their eyes followed the two predators' activity bit by bit, mouthful by mouthful of prey falling in the trap of teeth and disappearing a few moments later, the hyenas gazed more ravenously, swallowing their saliva, and fearing that their saliva would be the only thing to pour from throat to stomach. They were pacing left and right, taking small steps, but not daring to take one step forward.

Suddenly the lioness's pride collapsed, replaced by a strange feeling, leaving her the way consciousness leaves a cudgeled head. The body of that huge suffering - the suffering of being enveloped by senility - began to revive, rise up, and come to life. The lioness could not understand what was going on. She tried to push those unpleasant feelings from herself and continue breaking and tearing bones and flesh with more voracity, the only thing she could do, because the mouthfuls were their own excuse for passing down her throat. The lioness, arrogant, was begging in her heart, begging herself - according to her nature - to devour the gazelle till there was nothing left for the shameless, insolent hyenas. The male drew back from the colorful table as was his habit, and began licking his teeth and dark muzzle with his huge, wide tongue. This frightened the lioness. This meal must be food for many days, since that was all they ate. There was so much remaining and the lioness was getting full — because she was old — a beige beast, aging. Did that mean she had to leave her prey - the prey she had chased down with care and passion, fury and cruelty, and then had triumphantly torn apart — leave so the hyenas could get closer, then satisfy their lust before her eyes?

It was the first time she remembered her youth, because it was the first time she had thought of herself as old. In those days her victims could hardly calm her hunger. Her past passed before her and her revived suffering seemed a bigger and more predatory animal than she. And then she saw the hyenas emerging, as if they too had seen a beast more predatory than the lion. One crept over to the torn body of the gazelle - which still resembled a gazelle.

The hyenas attacked and fed their hunger, and their share which was greater than the loins'. Their unexpected happiness was obvious in their snorts and the short yips coming unbidden from their throats. The hyenas were eating, and their eyes were so filled with blood, flesh and bones that they did not see the lion, even out of the corners of their eyes. Finally, they could finish, until the gazelle was unrecognizable. And the vultures above their heads could land only when there was nothing on the bones except some shreds, unclear in sunken sun light as to whether they were flesh or merely blood clots drying.

The Hunted

Sour sweat ran along the fine hair on her scalp, tickling her skin, moving slowly toward her long eyebrows which shone brightly under the sun. Cautiously, slowly, like a statue avoiding reviving, she blinked and gazed again beyond the waves of long yellow grass to where a young deer was standing on thin, long legs. At that distance, it was hard to see it move. It took a while, so the young lioness, baking in the sun, became nervous. Her gums itched. Her teeth were clenched. She wanted to loosen her jaw and chatter so hard that the heart of the fragile young deer would crack. But she knew she shouldn't allow that, for the deer could sharply hear an even quieter sound, and then it might jump up sharply and run.

The young lioness was like a burning forest of fury, and she knew the wind of her thoughts would make the tongues of flame longer. She thought about her mother's last hunts when she was old. No bait could tire her; she never came back with a hanging head and drooping jaw, trying to forget. She might have been tired, but she always came back with her soul excited. If anything was pulling down her head, it would only be some heavy body she was dragging.

The young lioness tried to remember everything in detail. Flies were crawling near her nostril, sucking and tickling her. They wiggled in the cartilage of her ears and triggered her nerves. They were moving on her eyelids and were sometimes blown by the wind into her eyes, feeling like a sharp pencil moving side to side, cross-hatching her sight. She remembered – nothing should move her from her place; she should be a stone and come to life only when she could see a deer's leg muscles twitch.

And the young lioness saw the deer's leg muscles twitch. That was the moment. Her stony shell suddenly broke. Her muscles were vibrating at high frequency. She pushed all her fury into her toes, and sprang forward. Those toes could break grass stems even if they were trees. The deer jumped and ran when the lioness began her lethal attack. It ran happily before it knew the lioness was attacking. Soon it was running like a mass catapulted into space, and the young lioness was full of an anger that moved through her blood and her muscles like acid. She did not feel she was a lion, but a group of lions raging, splitting grass and air and time moving forward. The whole plain was too small for both of them, running like lightning after wind. The young lioness was not thinking anymore. She was nothing but a body, unstoppable until her claws would find her prey. This was not just hunting to fill the stomach – it had to embody a perfection that would calm her soul. Rolling her eyes, she imagined herself covered with deer blood, its smell satisfying the huge lust within her.

At the start, the deer and the lioness were running as fast as they could, as if they were running through empty space, worried about nothing. Would the wind get out of breath, or the lightning that followed? Both were hot, under the load of the sun. Both had lost count of their breathing, and their temperatures shot higher than the sun's. Suddenly the deer changed its direction; it was like a light shone directly into a mirror, a light the lioness could not take in. She could not see the deer. She became totally confused. Her paws were slipping and tangling – out of control – as if she had fallen in the mud. Her forward momentum could not be suddenly redirected when the deer leaped; her body bent so her tail swung in front of her face. In a single second something detached from her existence, something split within her – that very thing that had set her stare and made her a stone waiting in ambush for her young prey. The same thing that had thrown her legs forward and had triggered the image of the bloodstained deer behind her eyes. That same thing that made her feel she was several lions, not one. And now something else had replaced it; something which made her arms and legs slip and tangle, and made her dizzy. The very same thing that focused her eyes on the deer so far away.

She could no longer see its muscles twitching. She could see only the deer, but could not follow her. Her lungs burned as if the air were full of glass splinters making small, distracting wounds in her chest. Earlier, she felt no burning when running. But now everything had been changed by the deer. She was pure predator and violence. She would not admit she was less than her mother; her mother was old, while she was young. She had to start all over. She had lost speed and had to regain it. She had to return to the moment her stone shell was broken and her whole body energized. She stared at the deer with a gaze less sharp than before. It was further off than ever, further than at the beginning of the ambush. She latched her gaze onto the deer, and pushed herself along that sight line. She knew instinctively that tiredness will grip every runner's spirit, and that the young deer's chest was burning too. That idea increased her hope and whispered silently, "The deer is the one that must be breathless and exhausted, not you, the young lion hunter of a young deer." Not for a second did the consciousness, or the whisper, or the belief disappear. She ran faster every moment, matching her direction to that of the deer who turned sometimes right and sometimes left trying to confuse the lion. But the sight line between them kept the lion on track, running wherever the deer ran. She felt her power peaking in unbelievable speed, her body in the air more than on the ground. She was light as an eagle with wind under its wings. The goal: her claws in the deer's soft bottom, toppling it to the ground, and then the deer's neck broken in her teeth. That would be best.

But the deer was also reaching top speed, and its distance began increasing each moment, as the lioness's speed peaked and then fell. Little by little, the lioness was becoming aware of her body. The lightness was leaving, and heaviness in her muscles taking its place. She was now concerned with her running, and gasping for breath. Her gratifying rapture was about to crash, like the moment of satisfaction in every other lust. The deer was getting faster and the lioness was slowing down. The space became thicker for her as time went by; at first she was running in a vacuum, then she was surrounded by air, then paddling in water, then thrashing in honey, and eventually, the space she was running through turned into stone. The stone became the lioness's mold – she did not realize she had stopped. She thought herself still running. But she was as motionless as if she had never moved from her place. The sight line was lost, its hooks were released, and the deer shifted side to side a hundred times and was gone. The lion was there and the deer was not. What had her mother done that she did not do? Wasn't her body stronger? What did the old lioness have that she did not? Was her mistake at the beginning, when she leaped out from ambush?

She did not look anywhere, as if she was pretending she'd not been looking, as if she denied being a hunter stampeding her prey. Smells went through her nose of their own will. Strangers. Smells which made no image for her, left no memories, no signs, no paths. They only made her nod slightly – to the left, to the right, each way her neck could turn. Her ears followed her eyes; they wanted to hear where they were, as her eyes wanted to see where they were. The stone space returned to honey, water and air. Where had the deer been lost? She did not understand. But fear was flowing inside her, along with the smells in her nose, and the sounds in her ears, and also in her eyes through what she was seeing, fear, because she herself did not know where she was. How long had she run? Was she far from the plains, from the meadow? She did not know the smell of any plants, nor recognize any of the colors. There were trees she had never seen before, pointing at her, and nudging each other about the stranger. She shut her mouth, in deep withdrawal. She wanted to roar, but she was afraid – of everything, even of the grass she had trampled, even of the si-lence she heard among the tiny sounds, even of herself which felt so unfamiliar. She had never experienced such a situation. She was not being crushed anymore by the weight of the sun – another force was weighing on her back. Every way she looked, she saw the same things she had seen. Everywhere looked the same, as if there were mirrors repeating the place. She did not dare remember her mother, for then she would be like a lion cub lost. She was truly lost, but in order not to admit it, she would not think about her mother, or scramble to find her way back. She wished from her heart to rest, because her unrest came from her heart. Anything watching her would be a foe, seeing without being seen. She bent her legs and rounded her tail and slowly sat down, putting her paws forward, stretching out on the ground. She could not tell if her sitting was for relaxation or a sign of surrender. Nothing passed through her mind except the idea she had been trapped. It was not deer who did it. Who had set the trap? And was there a trap at all?

She sat there for a while, trying to sleep, thinking sleep might be a way out for her, and that she would find herself in grassland when she woke. The place – a bit further

– she could see her family here and there, her old father lying under the tree merged in stillness with its thick trunk. She could see her past in the dream – when she was a cub wrestling with her brothers and sisters, and her father with his big teeth would sometimes pick them up by the scruff and separate them. She could see her mother coming back from the hunt, with a bleeding animal between her teeth, tired but powerful. And after a while that warm flesh would be torn into pieces by the family members, and each piece had a different flavor, but they would all share the same smell and taste of blood.

She dreamed all these things while asleep. But when she opened her eyes, she was just there, in the same strange place. Even her father's big teeth would not have been able to separate her so from her previous life. Was it possible she would never see any of them again? Maybe she would not see lions until her death, or maybe even deer. As these things passed through her mind, she felt the air become colder; it was darker too. It was unclear where the sun was. It was lost, the same as the deer behind those trees and grasses. She had no more will. Her mind was absolutely empty – empty of any thought, any plan, any plot, any deception. She roared warily but her caution was hollow. There was nothing in her brain to consider. Her roar had no reverberation in space. She wanted to threaten the self hidden by that voice; but instead she voiced her own fear. She roared again and again; she was not giving up. She roared over and over with no will, like a branch shaken repeatedly by the blowing wind, its leaves rustling. She understood that her growls were nothing more than a rustling, but she continued nevertheless. She threw her head from side to side with every growl. This side, that side, everywhere the trapper might be hidden. But what trap? A trap as huge as a forest?

Her roars were soaring; each was a step

for the next to climb. Her whole body trembled from her own voice. Then she thought there was an enemy's hand involved, as if all were its agents; trees, grass, sounds, smells, cold weather, the sun sunken behind them. So she decided to fight. She forgot her mother and the vanished deer. She wanted only to vanquish her foe. She looked angrily at the trees, at the grasses and plants she did not know, and she thought of them – under her feet – as enemies waging battle with her toes. She ripped at them harder than she had ever torn apart a deer's body, and then attacked a tree, jumping to its trunk and climbing, as if she were looking for its face to claw. Her claws retracted, she fell to the ground and jumped to another tree. She was filled with insanity. Her wayward claws attacked everything without even wanting to. Her throat would not stop roaring and growling. Rising up against the trees, she hammered her head against their hard trunks, and did not feel the wounds on the thin skin of her forehead. Blood poured from her head to her brows, dripped into her eyes, came down the edge of her face, and flowed into her mouth. But the lioness did not weaken. In that sweet moment, there was a power in her madness which did not exist even at her top speed. She was fighting her own spirit and did not calm down till her opponent hit the ground and gave up. She continued even as her spirit receded step by step from her body. The darkness of the night also came step by step, swallowing the young lioness's body inside itself. The night stayed awake until the sun began to rise and the morning opened the dark. The lioness's body was spread out on the ground, and flies crawled in her nose and squirmed in her ears as if they were trying to learn the way to go and come back. The grasses, the stones and the trees remained in place, and all were spotted with dried blood.

To Be There

It's been a long time since they have sent a bill, as if they have forgotten I live here and use lots of water day and night, pull the curtains and turn on the lights. The tv is on indiscriminately, and summers and winters I don't vary the heater flame.

Yesterday I went to the warehouse to find a book. I did find it, but I couldn't take it off the shelf because there was a turtledove nest on the books with two chicks in it that didn't seem concerned with my arrival. Had I installed glass in the warehouse windows, it would not have happened. A glass cutter was nearby, down the alley next to the sta-tionary store. But now both of them have been made into a supermarket. If I want to buy glass, I won't be able to find it in a supermarket. So then I have to take a taxi and go much further from home.

Taking a taxi is too hard. A few days ago, I was in a taxi, "Exact change, please," he said. "Sure!" I said. I checked my pocket. "I don't have…" I said. "Oh dear!" he said, "Oh! I found some!" I said, "Thank god!" he said. "No, I was wrong. It was my keys". He laughed but I was not in a laughing mood.

For a long time, my belly hurts when I laugh, as if it had been stitched up. Everyone tells me to "go to a doctor", but my health insurance has long expired, and I've been healthy for a long time. Only once in mid-summer, Alireza took me to the pool and I caught a cold, but I didn't need to go to a doctor. I slept at home near the fireplace till I got better. Alireza visited me once, brought orange juice, put it in the fridge, and left. I did not move from my bed. After a while, the orange juice got rotten and I threw it away.

Every morning when I wake up, I tell myself that today, they'll turn off the water. Then I flip the light switch to see if the power is still on. Then I take a look at the fireplace flame and I worry that it won't stay lit till tomorrow! When I go to the warehouse too many unusable things have accumulated. It's been a long time since the scrap buyers' vans have come round, otherwise I would sell all that junk. In the warehouse, I can find some things, but I don't remember where I bought them. I found a photo glued to a wooden board, a landscape of a village. It is lush, with tall trees and mountains. Also you can see a lake in the distance, and ten or twelve houses. On the backside of the board, there is a half-torn paper sticker. On what's left is written "summer 1379"[3]. For sure, it had been the village name on the torn half. I thought it was a nice photo and took it from the warehouse. I put it on the table, leaning on the sugar-bowl. They were

3 Islamic calendar = 2000 AD Gregorian

not very thoughtful, attaching the photo to a board without a nail hole or a stand. I wanted to make a hole with a screwdriver, but I've been looking for a screwdriver for a long time and can't find one. My tool box is getting emptier day by day. I don't know where the tools are going. I saw there were no nails anymore, but there is no hardware store nearby. I'll let it lean on sugar-bowl for now. But the bad thing is when I want some tea I have to spoon the sugar slowly so that the board does not slide down, and I can't put the lid on the sugar-bowl, because it's difficult to pick it up, and if there is no lid, the sugar gets dirty. But it's better for me not to eat sugar.

Occasionally a neighbor brought me dried berries, and I ate them instead of sugar with my tea. It was really cool. But that neighbor left town one or two years ago, and a young couple moved here in her place, if they really are husband and wife. They don't know how the neighborhood works. They are not nice at all. They even don't say hello. I only see them going out sometimes and – if I am lucky and not asleep – coming back home. I watch them out the window. They see me sometimes. I wait for them to wave a hand or nod a head, but their look is colder than that. Even when I nod, but they look at me as if I'm spying on them. Maybe they're afraid of my eyes.

These days I am afraid myself as I look in the mirror because I am hollow-eyed, and my cheeks are so sunken, I chew them when I eat, and it hurts, and tears come, and my Adam's Apple is too protruding – as if I had swallowed a frog. Every day I find many white hairs on my head that I'm sure weren't there yesterday. It's so funny that although I am always in the house my skin is getting darker day by day. Little by little, I'm starting to look like a burnt match.

I don't know how long it takes for turtle-dove chicks to grow up. They have sat there, keeping twenty books from being read. I'm worried my glasses prescription will change before their time has come, so I won't be able to read the books under them with these glasses. I don't like changing glasses at all; it is more difficult than moving. I don't think about changing the tv channel as much as I used to think about moving. A house should not have rooms. I like my house to be like a loft, like a car showroom, so when I sit somewhere, I can see the whole house. A house that has one or two rooms makes you crazy. You worry constantly that somebody is in one of the rooms! You go to that room and look and find nobody there, and then you think maybe he is in the other room. You look inside the other one, but there's nobody there. You tell yourself maybe he was in the previous room and now he is in the living room. You come back into the hall, and see nobody. You tell yourself that surely he has escaped. Then you have to look carefully to see if anything has been moved from its place or not. Things are better now that I can lean this photo on the sugar-bowl; it is very loose and tends to slip. So I can be sure that if this photo has not moved, nothing else has been moved.

But these are all just delusions. One should move occasionally, or he will become delusional. When the turtledove chicks are gone and I can get my books, I will move. I will leave this district. There is nothing accessible here. I constantly have to take a taxi. But I am not so hopeful; Alireza said his district is just the same, as if everywhere is the same. I'd like to move somewhere different. Somewhere like the village in the photo. It's a good place. Every time I look at it, I would like to be there, I would like to live there. But first I have to know where it is. I have to show the photo to some people. Maybe they would know – if it has not changed since 1379. The unfortunate thing is that I never see anyone.

Moser

"Then we'll go to the amusement park, ok?" I said to him. He looked at me. His eyes were wet and lines of tears had dried on his cheeks. "Ok?" I asked. His lower lip was hanging. He didn't dare look at me anymore. "Walk faster, nephew!" I said. "I will, provided you don't put that buzzer on my head," he said. "Love you!" I said. He scuffed his small shoes against the asphalt so that his head shook when he walked.

"Wait!" I said him, as he pulled my hand and went ahead. "It's this way, honey! Where are you going?" I asked. "Not here, let's go somewhere else." "I love you..." I said, and pushed the glass door. "...Here is Naser's barbershop…" I held the door open with my bottom and hugged him. "You know how he likes you, don't you?" All the chairs were empty. Smiling, I said, "Hello Naser! How are you doing?" He looked at me and said, "Oh! What a surprise!" He picked up an apron, opened it, shook it out, folded it, and put it back in the same place. "Bring him over here," Naser said. "I had to force him to come," I said. My nephew looked at Naser, frowned, and pushed his face into my neck and shoulder. "What a nice boy! What's your name?" I looked down at my shoulder. He buried his face even more. His saliva soaked my shirt. "Say your name!... His name is… Want me to say it, or will you?... His name is Soheil," I said. "What a nice name! Come and sit here, Soheil. I want to make you beautiful. You're already beautiful…but more beautiful".

I walked toward the chair. When I wanted to put him down, he wrapped his arms around my neck and held tight. "Didn't we talk about this before? Mr. Naser will make fun of me if you don't sit down. He'll say: 'He won't obey you'". Soheil uncrossed his arms. I held my hands in his armpits and put him on the chair. He looked in the mirror for a while. Then his eyes started to turn toward the table. I knew what he was looking for. He pointed to the spray and asked, "What's that?" "That's a spray bottle. Don't be afraid, that's not it. He doesn't have it at all." He calmed down again.

Naser was washing his hands. He glanced at me in the mirror and asked, "Don't you want a trim?" I looked in the mirror. I ran my fingers through my hair like a comb. "Not necessary… is it?" I said. "As you wish. Why do you have a beard? Are you in mourning?" Naser asked. "No, is everyone who has a beard in mourning?" I asked. "And you're in black," he said. "No reason," I said.

He turned away from the mirror and looked directly at me. He shook his wet hands and went toward the rack. He dried his hands on a hanging towel, and then came up to Soheil. "You've gotten almost bald," I said to him, and took a seat. "Is there a problem?" he asked. He bent down and picked up a wooden plank. I got up immediately, put my hands in Soheil's armpits to lift him up. Naser put the plank on the chair arms. I put Soheil on the plank. Soheil was turning his head around, scanning the floor. I think he felt so high up. "No problem. Many people are bald. But you're a barber," I said. He laughed. I sat. Naser pushed the pedal with his foot and raised the chair a little higher. He looked at Soheil and me in the mirror and said, "He looks just like you." "Yeah, everybody says that," I said. Naser went to the drawer, opened it, and brought out a Moser with one hand, took its wire in the other and said to Soheil, "Do you have this toy?" Soheil cried, and was trying to see me at the side of the chair. I got up immediately and went toward him. He grabbed my neck tightly in his arms as I bent toward him. "Naser! You ruined it. I tried so hard to get him to come! He is afraid of that thing." Naser hit his forehead with hand and held it there for a while, thinking. Then he said, "So I'll trim you first."

I carried Soheil to the waiting seat and put him down. But he didn't let me stand up. He held my neck tightly. I looked in his honey-colored eyes with their two frowny eyebrows above them. "I'm going to get a trim; nothing to do with you. Ok?" I said. He calmed down. I put my lips on his soft, white cheek and squeezed them against it. They came back wet and salty. He opened his arms, and I picked up the plank and sat in the chair in front of the mirror. I tried to see him in the mirror but could see only the top of his head and his messy hair. Naser plugged the Moser into the socket near the mirror. "Let's have a cape," I said. I was looking into the mirror directly. I saw the pink cloth shake and close around my neck. Naser looked at me in the mirror from behind and smiled. There was nothing in his smile; it was empty.

Suddenly buzzzzzzzz…the Moser turned on. "Naser! Turn that off, man!" I said. "Looks like you're afraid too." He came toward me. The sound of the Moser went through my ears like a buzz saw. Naser picked up a comb from the table, put it above my ear, lifted some hair, and put the Moser to that. The vibration engulfed my whole head. It was like the sound of a motorcycle right up close. It sounded like revving the motorcycle when he moved it. The sound went around to the back of my head, the vibration too. They came around to my other ear little by little, all four of them; Naser, the comb, the sound and the vibration. Hit the gas again. The motorcycle sound. The motorcycle I was sitting on. Soheil was sitting in front of me where I always put some oily cloth. I tried to kiss his head. He shook his head and hit my nose too hard. I closed my eyes and grabbed my nose. Suddenly something hard hit us, and we went down –all three of us – me, Soheil and the motor-cycle – onto the ground. My foot was stuck behind the handlebars and I was pulled with the motorcycle along the asphalt. I saw Soheil rolling toward the stream like a watermelon. The street was swinging every-where like a boat on waves. Two feet were running toward my eyes. I closed them. Naser called, he was calling me. A cluster of thick hairs was sweeping up my face. "Get up! It's finished" Naser said. I rubbed my eyes with my hand and looked into the mir-ror. My head and my face were pruned like a tree. "Naser! Where is Soheil?" I asked. He did not answer. I just heard a deep breath. "I trimmed your beard just a little, because you said you were in mourning; it's not too short or too shabby." Naser said.

I looked into the mirror. "With that buzz-er?" he breathed deeply again. My eyes became wet, aimless. I looked into the mirror. All three of them were same color; all were black; my eyes, my beard and my shirt.

Read Carefully

The wicked people have increased.

Today I've seen one hundred wicked people.

They go through others

And come back through others,

But their teeth are made of metal. Their irises are made of Yemeni opal, and the whites of their eyes are made of limestone. Their bodies have germs all over. Their faces have germs. Their backs have germs. Their knees have germs, and they live among germs. The wicked people don't look at me passing by, or only when I look at them. When I ignore them, they bruise my face with their dazzled looks. They flow every day like the great river from the northernmost to the southernmost part of the city. Then they return via strong pumps. The flow is eternal and the great river will flow forever.

I always wanted to be one of the wicked people. To have metal teeth, to have opal & limestone eyes, and to have germs on my body. Because wicked people are the owners of laughter. They are the owners of loud laughter. They laugh as their alveoli rapidly fill and empty of air. For that reason, wicked people's alveoli have no germs. But I'm not like this. I am gradually getting like Bazargan's[4] photo, with the caption: "Where's your parrot, man? Died?" My laughter is not like loud laughter. And my alveoli are always full of air and rarely empty. So my alveoli are always swollen and bruised like a woman's cheek whose husband is always drunk and hitting her.

4 Bazargan means merchant. In Iranian folk stories a merchant usually has a parrot to watch his wife's relations when he is not home and is traveling. Bazargan also is the name of Iran's first prime minister after the Iranian revolution of 1979.

I am the literal translation of a "dark night in the bed", and anyone who sees me can realize everything's equivalent. Today after seeing one hundred wicked people I went inside the house and locked the door and closed the windows and closed the curtains. But the wicked people call, and if I don't pick up the phone, they will slip a piece of paper inside the house from under the door which says "Read carefully". And when I read it carefully, I gradually lose my attention until it's completely gone. They decrease my attention to zero. Then their alveoli fill and empty and I can hear it from behind the locked door, closed windows, closed curtains and unanswered phone. If the great river swelled out of its bed and took away my house, I wouldn't try to stop it. If my bowels were filled with the whites of their eyes I wouldn't worry – even if they gave my alveoli to their children to pop like bubble wrap.

But losing my attention is too awful. My attention is the only thing that separates me from my background. It is the only thing that makes me know I am me and I still exist. If I lost my attention it wouldn't make any difference which part of my body had germs, which part filled and emptied, or which part was made of opal and which of metal. A careless person's life could be made with scraps of wood, he could enjoy Haideh's songs and could run, shouting, reaching for the finish line. His worldview is as small as a newborn's scalp, and his heart is filled with squirt guns. I don't want to change to such creatures but I don't beg wicked people in this way since they don't feel pity for me. Today I send this request for other photos of Bazargan and other literal translations of "dark night in the bed", then I laugh out loud with my germy eyelashes and metal teeth and fill and empty my alveoli.

A Great Liar

It's something strange. These things are so strange. I've been thinking about these things for many years, so many years that I can't remember anything before them. I don't remember how young I was before I thought about these strange things! It is very strange, completely incomprehensible to me. Nobody can say how many men and women have seen it in their lifetimes; and I am just like them. I have seen many men and women and I have understood – by seeing them, and their talking, their laughing, their putting their hands under their chins, their putting their bags aside, their putting money in their pants pockets, their getting off and getting on, their crying, their calling, their wondering, their singing, their dancing, their climbing, their running, their smiling, their frowning, their thinking, their anger, their missing out, their eating food, their looking, their solving problems, their arranging a room, their caressing a kid's head, their shoving, and their gasping — that there is something called femininity. Certainly, I have met the word masculinity, but I did not understand it. I never knew what things symbolized masculinity. Is everything masculine unless it is feminine? Femininity is the strangest thing I have ever encountered.

When I was twelve, every day coming back from school, I walked along a long dirt road which was very lonely. Lonely means I see nobody except myself. There was sky and yellowish light-brown ground, and I was always plunged into fantasies. Most of the time a poem came to my mind, and I repeated it to myself so I wouldn't forget it.

When I got home, I tried to imagine the dirt road and the sky again, so as to have the same feeling when I would write.

After I don't know how many trips, I noticed a girl was also walking there. A girl walking on the same dirt road. At least I think she was a girl. She was walking ahead of me in a black headscarf, and if I wanted to catch up to her I would have to walk much faster, and probably I would reach her only after we had gone beyond the dirt road and gotten to a new asphalt street with buildings on both sides, and where suddenly the traffic of people and motorcycles and cars would have begun. And as I knew I could not say anything under those conditions, I would drop the idea and walk at the same distance.

I don't know how many days passed until the girl realized I was behind her every day and began looking back at me. The only thing that told me she had turned around was the contrast between the color of her face and her headscarf. Other than that, I could see neither her eyes nor her lips, nor even her nose very well. In the following few days, I noticed our distance had become less than before; I could see her eyes were light brown and her lips red, and her face white and bright. Once I thought I might have seen a half-smile.

I walked out every fifteen minutes after school until the academic year was over, and then I was home after those fifteen minutes. In the house I was as far from her as I was close to her during the school days. I walked behind her for something like two hundred days, fifteen minutes every day, and never talked to her. She was the source of inspiration for my poems. I was silent for about three thousand minutes, and lost the opportunity to talk to her. But I never blamed myself. This no-blame had three reasons. First; what was the point? Now she was gone and would never come back. Another reason: I used to feel that being friends with a girl – that most of the time starts by talking to a girl you do not know – is a big, unforgivable sin that would make all my good deeds worth nothing.

But the third reason: Though the first and second reasons seemed logical and sufficient, I was still blaming myself – and if the third reason did not exist, I would be a full-scale liar when I said "I never blamed myself." In fact, it was the third reason that was behind the sentence "I never blamed myself." The real story was that I thought for a long time about the girl who I would never see again, and I brought her to mind, and saw her just as I now see this pen and paper. During that time this was what I thought:

"I walked between 25 and 150 meters behind the girl. How could I know she was a girl? From her headscarf. Now suppose she had no headscarf. She might have worn a girl's or woman's dress, or perhaps a ladies' blouse or top. In that case I would have still understand she was a girl. Now suppose she had worn no female dress. Then maybe I would have understood she was a girl from the shape of her body, from her hips that were wider than boys' hips, and her shoulders that were more narrow. But suppose she had wider shoulders and narrower hips. In that case I would never have known if she was a girl in men's' clothing. Ok, suppose her hair had been short like boys'. Then what? Then it would have been impossible for me to know I was walking behind a girl. So the image of me walking behind a girl was only conceptual, and without the features I spoke of she had nothing to call me, as a boy, to become a girl's friend." But every time I review these thoughts and get to this point, another thought makes my head spin. This is the thought:

Suppose my conclusion is right, and without female features she had nothing which would present her as a girl who attracts me. But in this naive review, I jump over a very significant point. This jump causes facts to be concealed, and concealing the facts makes me think I have not made a mistake, and if I think I have not made a mistake it makes me calm and less likely to blame myself. What is that point?

Suppose the girl would have no dress at all and I would be only between 25 and 150 centimeters away from her, not between 25 and 150 meters, and she would have small hips and wide shoulders and her whole body would be just like a boy's. In that case, somebody who is looking for an excuse to avoid self-blame would have better and firmer reasons. But the main point that I should never jump over like a horse is that the girl turned around and looked back, and her look had a specific quality which pierced my heart, and her half-smile made my heart pound and beat faster. That look and that smile were absolutely feminine. I do not know the form of a masculine look and smile, but I understand that her look and her smile were feminine and her femininity was also in the way she walked, and in her slowing down which caused us to go from 150 meters to 25 meters. And every time I think about it this way, I blame myself. So the sentence 'I never blamed myself' is a great lie and I am a great liar.Femininity is something strange. It is not something to forget, it is not something easily lost, or replaceable by something else.

Wandering Spirit

I have been like that since childhood – I used to stay awake nights till late. And now I have gotten to the point where I sometimes stay awake till morning. Day does not have any of the strange power that night has over me. All day long I am languid and bored like a dog and I cannot count on me at all. But at night my mood is transformed, and I feel immeasurable energy, an energy responsible for how much I write, how many movies I watch, how many books I read, how much music I listen to without getting sleepy. Sometimes, my energy grows so much that I pace from side to side around the house and I think to myself and talk to myself constantly. I've always been like that. I guess I was twelve when my nightly insomnia began. Sometimes it crossed my mind to get out of house and run out into the silence of midnight, run until the sun rose and ordered: "That's enough! Go to bed".

I have never been scared of the dark. I do not put the darkness of night even in last place on the list of the scary things of the world. I never could understand people who were scared of the dark, or even people who are overcome by sleep as midnight comes on.

They say that staying awake at night causes premature aging and various subsequent diseases. I don't know, maybe it has happened to me, but it doesn't matter. If nature has enacted a stupid rule that everyone must sleep at night and that if they don't, it offers perfectly designed dire outcomes, then probably its plan is to deprive us of night. I think night is full of secrets and wonders that nature does not want us to know.

That's why it pours sleeping pills in our coffees. Despite all these cafés and all those coffees that they sell from day to night, there is still no one in the street at midnight and lights are off in every house.

I remember one of the nights I was awake – like every night – when I was twelve or thirteen – I heard the sound of bricks falling in the yard. In those days our yard was covered by coarse sand and we had built a kind of pyramid beside the restroom by piling bricks on one other. We had no goal in building that big pyramid, it was just because the bricks were there. I looked out through the window and in the dim alley power lights saw that some bricks had fallen down into the yard. We had laid a big wooden ladder against the wall next to the pyramid. Can you guess what I thought? It is obvious: I thought for sure a robber had come down the ladder and had imagined we had woken up when the bricks fell, and now he must be hiding somewhere.

He was wrong. The sound did not awaken anybody, but he did right to hide, because I was awake. I went slowly into the kitchen with bare feet, and in the pitch blackness – just by touch – I found a big knife and went toward the exit hallway, out onto the porch, and down the stairs. I looked everywhere the way policemen do in the movies. I turned suddenly and held the weapon up, threatening someone I thought might be there. There was nobody in the yard. But he might be in the outhouse.

The outhouse had no door, no toilet bowl, and no sink. It was only a dark brick structure full of barrels and masonry guide poles and planks. I walked step by step toward the outhouse unable to see anything in the dark. I went in and touched the walls and felt inside the barrels to make sure no one was there. When I came out, I looked into the underground cellar, now empty of the windows that must have been installed. Our cellar – in many people's opinion – was the scariest place of the world, and broke its own records for scariness at night. It was a home for cats, and for black, coarse hard-shell beetles that would come suddenly out of the earth. It was a fine place for a robber to hide because it was full of masonry equipment and barrels and darker than darkness itself.

Since I was determined to catch the robber, I walked barefoot slowly into the parking area, got to the cellar staircase at the end, and went down into the cellar with and without seeing, it did not matter. I moved my hands in the air and stepped cautiously ahead. My hand touched the barrels and oriented me. I felt inside the barrels to make sure no one was there. One of the barrels had fallen over and I found it with my feet. I bent over and crawled waist-deep inside, but nobody was in there. I walked to the far wall of the cellar and touched every corner, but no one was there. I came back through the same difficulties and got out outside again. The yard seemed so bright that it bothered my eyes. I guess until I die my pupils will never get as wide as they did that night. I did not find a robber. I looked at the bricks and I told myself, "Maybe it was a cat."

I guess I'm telling you this adventure to show how brave I was. Maybe because I'm not so brave now. Anyway, nights for me are the main time for living, and the words day, today, yesterday, nice day, days, up to date, daily news have no meaning for me. Instead, I am on the same wavelength with the words' night, tonight, last night, nightly, nightingale, nightmare, and half of the expression "day and night". My father called me a wandering spirit. Sometimes he used to say that he woke up last night and had seen me walking in the house like a wandering spirit.

History Book

How many days of your life so far have you spent thinking about impossible matters? Maybe it is an impossible matter – thinking about impossible matters, or that the earth – with no shrinking – passes through the eye of a needle – without the needle dilating. Or let's think about someone who is walking while he is standing. Or imagine doing unknown deeds – doing something without knowing why you should do it. Even you can think of seeing something that is neither lit nor emitting light. These all are considered impossible matters, and you stop thinking about them. But do you ever know how many impossible matters exist that we all stop thinking about? And why? Just because they are impossible. But think how many impossible things exist! How many! Don't they make you want to do something? They will stay impossible forever if you don't think about them. The compound noun "impossible matter" has kept them impossible and has made us shut down the possibility of making them possible.

Kissing someone who doesn't exist was once impossible, but it happens now. Now you believe you can kiss somebody who doesn't exist. I don't mean a kiss emoji on the unreal pages of computers and internet space. I mean the kisses which come from your lips actually sitting on someone else's lips, while neither of you exist. Breathing without lungs was impossible until a few hours ago, but now you see that you can breathe without fucking lungs, and even smoking is possible this way. You can walk on the roof and hang the light bulb from the floor. Weren't all of these once impossible?

I don't think it can go on like this – it's too boring. We are surrounded by impossible matters and we are only sitting around, happy with our conclusion, saying – with the look of a master to a disciple – "It's impossible." I don't accept it! I will never accept such words. Just look at history. History books can be found everywhere and you can easily read the historical facts. Finding a history book is not an impossible matter! Open the history book. The first things that catch your eye are ridiculous. You will laugh immediately and say: "Huh! How ridiculous!" you know why? You don't know yet, but when you open the history book you'll find out. But I'll tell you before that – you will say "ridiculous" because you will immediately come up against a "true" story about something impossible in the past. Something like unleashing the gorillas – it makes you laugh. Yes, once it was considered impossible to unleash black gorillas with their red furious eyes and their feet running on the ground on their palms.

History is full of phenomenal happenings: weaving carpets, repairing small brass locks, anthems, glossy paper sequins, licking a lollipop standing next to a tower; they have filled history, these weird things that are sometimes ridiculous to read about, and sometimes shake your body with fear.

One Paragraph Ago

We do not reach out to anything, we do not go anywhere, we do not come from anywhere, and do not get away from anything unless with hands and feet. Hands and feet are everything in this life. Every time I look at the sky, I think to myself, "How great hands and feet are!"

Humans' hands and feet work just like their brains and even better. I know someone who has a house in London and is the owner of an entertainment, sport, amenities, cultural, artistic, scientific complex in the United States, and another just like it in Iran. She has one daughter, two sons and another daughter, all completely successful. They are in the top of their elementary education classes, and they are headed for a bright future. Her husband is a devoted man – good-looking, slim and fit, from a wealthy family (he is the son of a famous Hollywood director I prefer not to name), brainy, stylish and a unique character in most of life's affairs. But his devotion is greatest to his wife. Apart from her family, she is a very successful person. She has won the woman of the year award repeatedly, and her face has appeared on magazine covers. A personal helicopter, a yacht, four great villas in four countries – the Netherlands, France, Italy and Belgium – with four luxury cars with their drivers, and a great span of Mediterranean beaches are a few of her properties. Even luck and the hand of heavenly powers support her – that's why she won all the lottery prizes. Every time she wishes to live better, her wish is fulfilled and she lives better. People have repeatedly observed a big stone falling suddenly from the sky right toward her remaining suspended in the air as it gets close to her – until she takes one step forward or back or right or left or left-back or right-back or left-forward or right-forward. No doubt you all understand who I am talking about, and you know her well. Each one of you, male or female, old or young, intelligent or insane – no matter how happy you feel living in your house or your apartment or your cardboard box – in the depth of your heart, where your voice cannot reach even your mind's ear, you would say: "I wish I were she!"

But do you realize that her life without hands and feet would be worth nothing? Or if you had her life without hands and feet it would be worth nothing? Or if everybody had her life without hands and feet it would be worth nothing? No, we do not realize this, and are not even aware of our igno-rance while we have hands and feet, yet we complain about suffering. But at this point in my life, I have concluded that nothing in this world is better than hands and feet. I have learned the path of wisdom from hands and feet. Presidents, butchers, librarians, researchers, downtown retailers, drug dealers, florists and ladies all are following the path of wisdom. And I have been on this path since I figured out the dignity of hands and feet. In the time it takes one paragraph to go by.

When you are standing on a stone bench, think about hands and feet. When you are fighting in a war, think about hands and feet. When anesthesiologists stand ready next to your bed, think about hands and feet. If you might have to apologize to someone, think about hands and feet. If you want to pass rest of your life differently, think about hands and feet. When you laugh, think about hands and feet. When you kiss someone, think about hands and feet. When you are called sir, madam, engineer, doctor, boss, Mr., Captain, Master, dude, fellow-citizen, brother, excellency, your excellency, dear father, baby, darling, neighbor, guy, or even hey, you – only think about hands and feet. When you think, think about hands and feet and never give up hands and feet for anything.

All in all, these are not some things someone taught me to repeat like a Myna-bird. These are things I did not know for my whole life and in my lifetime second by second, and I reached out to them just two paragraphs ago. After reading this, if you might want to say something, think about hands and feet.

Recorded News

A few times a day the news is broadcast on tv. The first news comprises new news that is on the mind of the viewer, and the listener quickly and easily arranges the news in order. New news lines up and observes the order neck and neck. All news is silent and even if a bee is going to sting one new news' nose, it doesn't turn to look, let alone kill it or make it fly away. Listeners enjoy the order and silence of the news. They feel joy in complete ignorance and in the very deep layers of their unconscious. Surely you've experienced the joy of someone massaging your shoulders, back and feet. As when somebody is massaging your mind, this is the joy of awareness. Awareness is an extra-terrestrial, extra-material, and generally extra- feeling that can't be described. That's because if you are aware, you can talk with self-confidence, and when you are interrupted by someone, you stare into his eyes and say, "As you see, I'm explaining." Even if someone else is talking to you, when you are aware, you can safely nod your head and complete every sentence he says.

But beyond the first news that spreads new news, there is more news broadcast every day, a record of new news called recorded news. Most people aren't interested in recorded news, because recorded news repeats the new news, news which was already silently there in the minds of viewers and listeners earlier. There's no more space for more news in the mind of the viewer and listener, especially for news which is exactly like the previous news. If you had a supermarket, and biscuits from a, β and ح companies are supplied to you, would you want the same biscuits supplied by other companies? Or imagine Hessam Habibi and Abo Shayeq Hakami are invited to your house, each being entirely themselves. An hour later the doorbell rings, and when you open the door you see Hessam Habibi and Abo Shayegh Hakami at the door. Will you invite them in? They are already your guests, and now one of them is sleeping and the other is taking a shower.

This is the reason why people don't like recorded news. And this unpopularity makes recorded news sad. Recorded news is angry indeed. It can't accept not being accepted by most people. Its feeling seems irrational, but you are human beings. Please have more feeling and give things a second look. Put yourselves in the place of record-ed news for a minute and see how grievous it is when no mind is ready to accept you in its space. And many times you hear, "Ugh! This is recorded!" Like when you ask your spouse to pay attention to what you are saying, and she replies, "Go away. You have nothing new for me. I spent twenty years with someone just like you in my previous life." It's ok with me if you commit suicide. But recorded news is not as dull as you are.

Recorded news tolerated this disgrace for years, and when it couldn't find a cure, decided to do something to change its fate instead of using potassium cyanide, a razor in the bathtub, or a four-story building. It knew nobody could do it but itself. One sunny day, when it was being broadcast some hours after the new news, it did something wonderful. It changed itself. Yes, it changed itself so that it had no similarity to the new news. It didn't pay attention to the first news broadcast a few hours ago, and it broadcasted news different from the first news. Recorded news did something new with a furious face and a dynamic voice full of self-confidence, and it felt itself free for the first time, as if there was nothing to make it stop. Like an image in a mirror separated from its source and acting independently, like a mountain echo in which plays some different music, it proved it was not just a vain copy of the original that is the first news. It could cast its own sound and images onto the tv screen.

Recorded news now has news which belongs to it alone. Now it hesitates about one of these three: potassium cyanide, a razor in the bathtub and a four-story building. After understanding that its lack of popularity is not due to its similarity to the new news, it has decided to end its life with one of these methods. Besides this bitter truth, there are two other bitter reasons that recorded news can't be set free. First, recorded news is not first, it is always broadcast after the new news and not to be first is recorded news's main problem. Second, its name: recorded news is never a suitable name for a creature that wants to assert its uniqueness. The four-story building scares it. It has heard a lot about the tranquility of death by potassium cyanide, but still isn't sure about it. Death by razor in the bathtub would make for better graphics. Recorded news is sure the news of its suicide would be broadcast in the new news.

Unrivaled and Sensational

A house is not a place to live, a house is a place for sleeping to death, a house is the worst place in the world, nothing is beautiful in a house, nothing is lovely in a house, nothing is good in a house – if the house doesn't have a kitchen. Everything starts in the kitchen. When I say everything, I mean everything that's good. In a kitchen, there are both fridge and oven, so there is both ice and fire. There is fruit and cold water in the fridge and hot food in the oven. There are dishes in the kitchen, tea is in the kitchen, cocoa, chocolates, and nuts and drinks are all in the kitchen. The kitchen is the best place in the world, and the world has so many of these best places.

I knew a boy who had fallen in love with a thin, lonely girl. The girl was silent and her face was fascinating even when the boy could not get close. At first, the boy's interest was just like any male interest in any female – like the attraction of a couple of flies to one another, like the draw of two opposite poles of a magnet, like Adam and Eve. But after some time passed, and the boy knew the girl more and could predict her reactions in different situations, and had experienced the girl's strange, unexpected behavior, he realized: "Wow! This girl can really make somebody fall in love with her!" This sentence had not yet formed in his mind, but when he looked in his heart, he saw the little seed of love sprouting. There was no difference from what the boy had wanted before. But now he had fallen in love with a thin, lonely girl, and had no other choice but to reach her.

Days and weeks passed, and the boy, unaware of the costs he incurred, and the suffering he had, was trying to join her, and nothing except the heavy sorrow of separation worried him. He loved the girl so much that he wished there was nobody in the world except for the girl. But that was not the case. There were so many girls in this world; the girls were silent, their attractiveness made boys afraid of getting close, and girls' reactions were unexpected and totally unpredictable. The girls were thin, the girls were lonely…but that one lonely thin girl was the only girl he loved, who he wanted to be with in his heart. No girl could replace her.

No matter how the boy tried, over years and years, nothing came of it but a broken heart and sorrowful memories. I was just trying to say there is a lot of kitchen - which is the best place in the world – in this world. But there is only one kitchen which is unrivaled and sensational, just like the lonely thin girl, and the mourning of its eyes affects the heart of every living thing through falling-in-love. That kitchen is our kitchen, a kitchen that has a light illuminating everything in it. This light is a lamp which is just like the sun – round and warm and bright. Its only difference is that while the sun is always on, the lamp switches on and off with a single switch on the wall. This switching on and off is the lamp's advantage over the sun.

When the kitchen light is turned on, light shines into the hall and foyer. The light will shine into the bedroom if the door is open. Its light will shine in the alley too, and will make it entirely light if we pull the curtain aside. This light will also shine into the neighbors' house if they pull their curtains aside – shining there so brightly that they can even read books. The reflection of this light from the windows of nearby buildings reaches almost everywhere in the city. One can't find anywhere bright, unless it's lit by our kitchen light. Our kitchen light makes the whole city bright; it shines on the side streets so cars can drive without turning their lights on. It travels on to every region and country; no region or country is without our kitchen light. Our kitchen light makes the world bright all around, brighter than as the sun, which lights only half the world at any time.

When the night is over, we turn the kitchen light off, and the world sinks in darkness. The sun rises, but how much light does it give? People lose their way and become confused in the darkness, and robbers take this opportunity to pick pockets. The people complain to the police, but how can the cops find the robbers in the darkness? The people shop, but they buy the most inferior and corrupt stuff from sellers because in the darkness they can't see what they are buying, what they are eating, where they are going, what they are doing, what they are giving, what they are taking, what they are becoming.

In the half-year that nights are longer and our kitchen light stays on more, the world situation is better. The people are fine and the world orbits according to human will. But most people do not know this. Most people are unaware of the fact that it's our kitchen light. They would probably say "What's the difference between your kitchen and other kitchens?" That is when I have to tell them the story of the boy who fell in love with the lonely thin girl.

As a Bud Blooms

It's not at all right to think about a good and comfortable life. I am sure it is noticed in the heavenly books – it has to be. Because it is a bad business indeed. It's like a lonely boy thinking all day about the girls he saw. It's like a diabetic thinking about all kinds of candy. It's like a canary thinking about flying while it is in a cage. A human who has a bad and uncomfortable life should not think about a good and comfortable life because these thoughts don't make him try – little by little – to save himself from that situation. And also, they make him try to find the fastest and easiest way to success.

One was from the midlands and another one was from the south. Both were homeless and displaced. They found each other in a foreign country listening to one another's stories. That is one of the bad deeds too, because it makes you enjoy hearing about someone else's sorrows, and seeing your sorrows as greater when hearing about someone else's happiness. They did it anyway, and told each other about their sorrows and happinesses, great and small. As is usual in such cases, something happens which has a name: "friendship". Yes, they became friends. The friendship of a midlander and a southerner must be weird, but sharing stories makes something weirder possible: that weirder thing is "comradeship". They became comrades and decided to do something to help end their bitter lives. They each had been capable of committing suicide, but that was for a time when they were lonely. Now each of them had a companion comrade who increased their hope for staying alive.

So instead of suicide, they decided to steal. Stop blaming them, and don't bite your lip! If you would think about a good and comfortable life in the same way as these two people did, you would make the same decision. Have you ever heard that hopefulness and effort and cooperation are the effective factors in reaching success? What you have heard is exactly right. With hopefulness and effort and cooperation they could rob a jewelry store and escape. But it's so easy to be lost in a foreign country. They got lost in the dark night just like two mosquitos, and the law officers' efforts made them even more confused. They ran a lot here and there until they found themselves alone in some quiet village. They had no idea where they were. It was quite late at night when they arrived and found a ruined, abandoned house to rest in. "Let's just sleep here," Midlander said. "Right here?" Southerner asked. "Yes, right here," Midlander said. "Why?" Southerner asked.

"Because I'm sleepy," Midlander said. "But I can't sleep," Southerner said. "You can if you lie down on the ground," Midlander said. "I'm afraid to," Southerner said. "Don't be afraid," Midlander said. "Will you fall asleep soon?" Southerner asked. "Yes," Midlander said. "Is your sleep deep?" Southerner asked. "Yes," Midlander said. "Aren't you afraid?" Southerner asked. "No," Midlander said. "So please wait until I fall asleep, and then you can go to sleep!" Southerner said. "If I can," Midlander said, and his eyelids got heavy as they lay down on the ground. "Are you asleep?" Southerner asked. "Not yet," Midlander said. "Don't fall asleep! Let me go to sleep first, please!" Southerner said. "Ok, try to sleep soon, I'm dead tired," Midlander said. "How can you sleep safely?" Southerner asked. "With eyes closed and open mouth." He said that and his eyelids fell. "Are you asleep?" Southerner asked. Midlander said with a faltering voice, "No…." "Don't sleep!" Southerner said. " I'm awake," Midlander said and then sniffed. "Did you fall asleep?" Southerner asked, but this question never got answered because Midlander had fallen asleep so deeply that he didn't wake up until morning.

But in the morning, sleep was over, and Midlander woke up as quietly as a bud blooms – and found himself alone in that wreckage. Southerner was not there. It was worrying. But the absence of the gold – that was more worrying. He discovered immediately that the Southerner had taken the gold and run away. It's so easy to be lost in a foreign country. The Southerner had gotten lost in the dark night like a mosquito, and Midlander's efforts to locate him made himself more confused. This idea that Southerner had run away with the gold was not Midlander's pessimism, because he quickly remembered all Southerner's words the night before, and he understood the meanings he had not thought of last night; 1. Will you fall asleep soon? 2. Is your sleep deep?

3. Aren't you afraid? 4. So please wait until I fall asleep, and then you can go to sleep! 5. How can you sleep safely? This last one set Midlander's heart on fire. In fact, Southerner was afraid of betraying his friend. That's why he wanted to go to sleep before him. But Midlander's sleep, made them both miserable; one lost his honor and the other lost his share of the gold.

I guess you can understand now why it is not right to think about a good and comfortable life – when life is bad and uncomfortable. Conversation is not good either. Nor are friendship and comradeship. Hopefulness and effort and cooperation are also bad. There are too many bad things, and too few good ones, very few, so rare that it is never possible to have a good and comfortable life with them.

The Effect of a Very Strong Coffee

"The soldiers are gone. They've been gone for a long time." The person saying this doesn't understand soldiers. He knew the soldiers only from their uniforms. But the soldiers have to be known for what is going on in their hearts – not their heads. Like the one standing behind the door. The stupid boy said again, "The soldiers are gone. I saw them leaving. They carried flags." The young girl did not answer, and was brushing her hair. The soldier kicked in the door, and did not look at either of them. His gaze was shifting here and there. But the young girl and the little boy looked at him. A convulsive and awful look; which one's look was like that? The soldier was rude, but the boy's rudeness was greater. His extreme fury caused the soldier to react to the beating of his small fists by laying him out with several blasts of his gun. But what had made him a soldier were not these inevitable blasts. He was a natural-born soldier. Like an axe whose life will be completed by a tree falling. Like a male that finds his existence riding on a female. The young girl screamed loudly. Her scream sounded like blood suspended in a vein, the sound of suddenly chewing one's tongue at a meal. What dedicated soldier could tolerate such a sound? A simple shot would have been enough. But three shots to just one point of her forehead was satisfying, as satisfying as the instinctive muscle release after escaping from the cold and getting close to a flickering fire.

Then there were two bodies and one big soldier who looked at neither of them. Why? He has to look at them! He has to enjoy watching them and sucking his lips between his teeth with lust. But he did not do that. He stood and thought – an absurd, false thought. A thought without light. A unique silence that was not annoying but was formed by annoyingness. "The soldiers are gone. They've been gone for a long time. They carried flags!" The stupid little boy said that sentence one more time. He had said it earlier one more time for the others . A young girl was sitting on the sofa playing with the teeth of her plastic comb. There were so many windows whose business was transparency, with their backs to the light and facing the darkness. Everybody walking in front of them could be described as a curtain against the light – visible and invisible.

The aged colonel's caper on the other side of the windowless wall was changing everything. He – at that age - could not overcome his bladder. The little boy touched the young girl's hair, and the girl pushed back his hand and continued combing, and the boy shot the girl a look full of frustrated masculinity, and subjection of his lust.

The colonel kicked in the door and – it must be known – with the speed of a real soldier, got rid of his belt, pulled down his pants and sat on the toilet, a fine place to bury them. They looked at each other and thought this tree probably needs manure. That's why they – with no consultation, and with ridiculous imagination vibrating in both their heads – dug out the dirt under the tree and buried the dead sparrows. The last time they looked at the sparrows, their hearts had ached, it was misery, for they weren't hardened soldiers. The old man was watching them from the other side of the yard rubbing skin moistener on his hands. What was he dreaming about? He rubbed until the mosquito on his neck could per-fectly accomplish its bloodsucking mission.

The soldier looked at the young girl's body. It was her hair that fascinated him, and unfortunately, he was not cruel enough to enjoy inspecting the holes on her forehead. The girl's dark brown hair was blood-stained and oddly colored, and as he stared at that color, the strangest feeling pulsed through the soldier's troubled body.

Everything was on schedule. He had read all the books. All the books in that library were full of tiny living creatures that had made some place like a walkway on the illustrated pages. They too were afraid of redemption, because the chemically smelly stuff would make them suffer so much the redemption would not be worth it. She hid behind him and he was the first one who had nobody in front to hide behind. More than ten bodies were in the trench behind him and he was under a layer of air that was entirely transparent. It was that layer of the air that was protecting him when the gunfire began. It was compressed much like an iron rock, heavy, dense, but transparent and ethereal. Under all those hands waving overhead – the shoulders ended in a neck with a shouting, moving head above it – he was seeing his photo and smiled. He was filled with great fear, but which things before his eyes made him smile? Those ebullient, hopeful faces? Or his own reliably happy face in the photograph? It took only a little time to understand that it was the specific images of the future reviving in his head that made him smile. He recognized his own medium-size body in the figure of a president standing behind a tribune that was the center of tens of spherical and cubic and cylindrical microphones; he knew perfectly that beautiful face.

The stupid little boy was still punching the soldier's belly, and the heavy soldier whose cruelty was part of his existence – not for this reason but for thousands of reasons – was scratching and grinding and ruining that existence by petting the boy's stupid head. The boy calmed down and looked at the soldier. The young girl gazed at the soldier's eyes that stared at the little boy's eyes. They shone together and made each other bright, and the little boy watched the reflection of the young girl's look in the overwhelmed soldier's eyes and his newly ripened masculinity began to emerge.

The old man – while he was still creaming his hands – told the kids around him that it was the first period. "Which?" one of the kids asked, and he answered: "When the deer's eyes will be the first part of its body to feed the soil bacteria." We looked at each other. We loved each other. We were falling in love with each other just as in the past when we were simple, thoughtless teens. When I first saw her, a giant bell rang twelve disordered times through my flesh, and I understood that I would love her. What a sweet love that was! Like when only one person could be loved. Like when a child has lost his ball and until his death – when he is not a child anymore – he wants that very ball, and not another. We were looking at each other, and signaling. The same as two soldiers must signal. Two bold, dutiful soldiers – even if one is male and the other female. We were leaving all the speeches unheard, and the delusion of success had made us wet and aqueous, and we were stepping heavily.

The blood on that dark brown hair would impress any headstrong young man. Everybody was looking and attracted to that unmatched picture, as if they were going to worship but did not know which – the girl? Or the blood? Or the dark brown hair? Or the three images merged into one? Or all of them? It was a crime called polytheism.

The sparrows were buried under the shadow of the tree, and I tried to dig them out of my partner's eyes with my newly cut nails. But the terrible truth was that I did not know what to do next. It was my shameless ignorance that kept me from being a sol-dier. This is a bitter story: that I can never – as long as I live – be a soldier. Soldiers are recognized by their uniforms. But my heart does not embrace them. I was completely a civilian, with the same clothes, stature and age as the bodies that had three hearts – one behind the chest bone and two on their sleeves. It is a difficult business. We can never hide this secret behind our naive eyes. When the secret flies from one's eyes to the other's, it fills the atmosphere with its strange odor, quickens the noses of dogs, and releases their barking all over the garden. Then everybody comes toward us. We run away, and run, and try to get away. But they who run behind us are trained for such situations – even their breathing does not get faster – not an official training in a specific period of their lives, but an eternal education.

My dear children! I am not here to speak. I am here to finish off the effect of the coffee, the coffee that the writer drank last night and was sickened by its thickness. That strong coffee caused a dissonant madness that glued his eyes to the paper and made his stomach jump. Now it is my duty to do away with the effects of the coffee, though that horrible condition persists in his head. Its resistance won't last, and I am here to announce with confidence that everything is over. Everybody who wants to can be anyone. Everything is over.

More story collections from Fomite...

MaryEllen Beveridge — *After the Hunger*
MaryEllen Beveridge — *Permeable Boundaries*
Jay Boyer — *Flight*
L. M Brown — *Treading the Uneven Road*
L. M Brown — *Were We Awake*
Michael Cocchiarale — *Here Is Ware*
Michael Cocchiarale — *Still Time*
Neil Connelly — *In the Wake of Our Vows*
Catherine Zobal Dent — *Unfinished Stories of Girls*
Zdravka Evtimova — *Carts and Other Stories*
John Michael Flynn — *Off to the Next Wherever*
Derek Furr — *Semitones*
Derek Furr — *Suite for Three Voices*
Elizabeth Genovise — *Where There Are Two or More*
Andrei Guriuanu — *Body of Work*
Zeke Jarvis — *In A Family Way*
Arya Jenkins — *Blue Songs in an Open Key*
Jan English Leary — *Skating on the Vertical*
Marjorie Maddox — *What She Was Saying*
William Marquess — *Badtime Stories*
William Marquess — *Because Because Because Because Because*
William Marquess — *Boom-shacka-lacka*
William Marquess — *Things I Want You to Do*
Gary Miller — *Museum of the Americas*
Jennifer Anne Moses — *Visiting Hours*

Martin Ott — *Interrogations*

Christopher Peterson — *Amoebic Simulacra*

Christopher Peterson — *Scratch the Itchy Teeth*

Charles Phillips — *Dead South*

Jack Pulaski — *Love's Labours*

Charles Rafferty — *Saturday Night at Magellan's*

Ron Savage — *What We Do For Love*

Fred Skolnik— *Americans and Other Stories*

Lynn Sloan — *This Far Is Not Far Enough*

L.E. Smith — *Views Cost Extra*

Caitlin Hamilton Summie — *To Lay To Rest Our Ghosts*

Susan Thomas — *Among Angelic Orders*

Tom Walker — *Signed Confessions*

Silas Dent Zobal — *The Inconvenience of the Wings*

Writing a review on social media sites for readers will help the progress of independent publishing. To submit a review, go to the book page on any of the sites and follow the links for reviews. More reviews help books get more attention from readers and other reviewers.

For more information or to order any of our books, visit:
http://www.fomitepress.com/our-books.html